ALCOHOL

by Michael V. Uschan

DRUG
EDUCATION
LIBRARY

Lucent Books, San Diego, CA

To Bill W. and Dr. Bob, the founders of Alcoholics Anonymous.

Library of Congress Cataloging-in-Publication Data

Uschan, Michael V., 1948–
   Alcohol / by Michael V. Uschan.
      p.   cm. — (Drug education library)
   Includes bibliographical references and index.
   Summary: Discusses the history, effects, health and
social aspects, and legal ramifications of alcohol, as well
as treatments for alcoholism.
   ISBN 1-56006-911-2 (hard : alk. paper)
   1. Alcoholism—Juvenile literature. 2. Alcoholism—
Treatment—Juvenlie literature. 3. Alcoholism—
Prevention—Juvenile literature. [1. Alcohol. 2.
Alcoholism.] I. Title. II. Series.
   HV5066 .U83 2002
   362.292—dc21

                                        2001003772
2001004069

Copyright © 2002 by Lucent Books, Inc.
10911 Technology Place, San Diego, CA 92127
Printed in the U.S.A.

Contents

Foreword

The development of drugs and drug use in America is a cultural paradox. On the one hand, strong, potentially dangerous drugs provide people with relief from numerous physical and psychological ailments. Sedatives like Valium counter the effects of anxiety; steroids treat severe burns, anemia, and some forms of cancer; morphine provides quick pain relief. On the other hand, many drugs (sedatives, steroids, and morphine among them) are consistently misused or abused. Millions of Americans struggle each year with drug addictions that overpower their ability to think and act rationally. Researchers often link drug abuse to criminal activity, traffic accidents, domestic violence, and suicide.

These harmful effects seem obvious today. Newspaper articles, medical papers, and scientific studies have highlighted the myriad problems drugs and drug use can cause. Yet, there was a time when many of the drugs now known to be harmful were actually believed to be beneficial. Cocaine, for example, was once hailed as a great cure, used to treat everything from nausea and weakness to colds and asthma. Developed in Europe during the 1880s, cocaine spread quickly to the United States where manufacturers made it the primary ingredient in such everyday substances as cough medicines, lozenges, and tonics. Likewise, heroin, an opium derivative, became a popular painkiller during the late nineteenth century. Doctors and patients flocked to American drugstores to buy heroin, described as the optimal cure for even the worst coughs and chest pains.

As more people began using these drugs, though, doctors, legislators, and the public at large began to realize that they were more damaging than beneficial. After years of using heroin as a painkiller, for example, patients began asking their doctors for larger and stronger doses. Cocaine users reported dangerous side effects, including hallucinations and wild mood shifts. As a result, the U.S. government initiated more stringent regulation of many powerful and addictive drugs, and in some cases outlawed them entirely.

A drug's legal status is not always indicative of how dangerous it is, however. Some drugs known to have harmful effects can be purchased legally in the United States and elsewhere. Nicotine, a key ingredient in cigarettes, is known to be highly addictive. In an effort to meet their bodies' demands for nicotine, smokers expose themselves to lung cancer, emphysema, and other life-threatening conditions. Despite these risks, nicotine is legal almost everywhere.

Other drugs that cannot be purchased or sold legally are the subject of much debate regarding their effects on physical and mental health. Marijuana, sometimes described as a gateway drug that leads users to other drugs, cannot legally be used, grown, or sold in this country. However, some research suggests that marijuana is neither addictive nor a gateway drug and that it might actually benefit cancer and AIDS patients by reducing pain and encouraging failing appetites. Despite these findings and occasional legislative attempts to change the drug's status, marijuana remains illegal.

The Drug Education Library examines the paradox of drugs and drug use in America by focusing on some of the most commonly used and abused drugs or categories of drugs available today. By discussing objectively the many types of drugs, their intended purposes, their effects (both planned and unplanned), and the controversies surrounding them, the books in this series provide readers with an understanding of the complex role drugs and drug use play in American society. Informative sidebars, annotated bibliographies, and organizations to contact lists highlight the text and provide young readers with many opportunities for further discussion and research.

 **Introduction**

It Touches Everyone

Most people who drink alcoholic beverages suffer no ill effects. They drink moderately with meals and in social settings. "For most people alcohol is a pleasant accompaniment to social activities. Moderate alcohol use is not harmful for most adults,"[1] says the National Institute of Alcohol Abuse and Alcoholism (NIAAA).

In the United States, two-thirds of adults drink alcoholic beverages at least occasionally, a figure that is similar to consumption patterns in other nations. For most drinkers, alcohol is an enjoyable addition to many facets of their daily lives; it creates no problems and does not endanger their health.

For a small percentage of people, however, drinking can be dangerous. These drinkers run a very high risk of becoming addicted to alcohol. John Lawson, in *Friends You Can Drop: Alcohol and Other Drugs,* explains that this human malady, known today as alcoholism, is an ancient one:

> The alcoholism syndrome is one of man's oldest afflictions, cited in his earliest writing, a source of misery and lingering death that has remained a constant over the centuries. Other devastating, epidemic illnesses have been conquered and have moved into the realm of medical history. [But] alcoholism has remained, blighting the human condition, and its pattern today is identical to that experienced by its victims in the ancient world, the Middle Ages, the Renaissance, and the Industrial Revolution. It is timeless and knows no barriers.[2]

The reality of alcohol use in the twenty-first century is that tens of millions of people throughout the world drink so much alcohol that it is destroying their lives. In 2001 the NIAAA reported that nearly 14 million Americans, 1 in every 13 adults or 7.4 percent of the total population, abused alcohol or was an alcoholic. The World Health Organization estimates that as many as 140 million people globally are harming themselves because they drink too much.

Why some people can consume alcohol moderately all of their lives while others have trouble quitting the first time they take a drink is a question that has long puzzled humankind. Scientists have now identified several factors that make it more likely for a person to develop a drinking problem, the most important of which is heredity—a person's genetic makeup will determine how

Alcoholic beverages are often consumed during social gatherings.

Having passed out from drunkenness, a mother is unable to care for her child.

they react physically to alcohol. The link between heredity and alcoholism is undeniable, as shown by the high percentage of children of alcoholics who later develop drinking problems.

Alcohol Affects Everyone

Alcohol touches the lives of many people, even those who never take a drink. In the United States, for example, more than one-half of Americans and one-quarter of all children younger than eighteen have a close family member who is alcoholic. Nearly everyone at some time in their life will come in contact with a person who drinks too much, whether it is a friend, coworker, classmate, or a stranger they encounter in a restaurant or other setting. It is because alcohol use touches the lives of drinkers and nondrinkers alike that it is important to understand how this drug works.

Chapter 1

A History of Alcohol Use

A lcohol is a clear, thin, odorless liquid that is produced by fermentation. Fermentation is a chemical reaction that occurs naturally when yeast, a microscopic plant that floats freely in the air, reacts with food that contains sugar. Fruits and berries have sugar in the form of fructose, which ferments as they become overripe due to yeast. Grains from wheat, rye, and barley also have natural sugars that can be transformed into alcohol as they age. Birds can become drunk from eating such fermented foods, and biologists have observed that animals in the wild sometimes become intoxicated in the same way.

How or when people first discovered how to control the fermentation process is unknown. However, historians know that people have been drinking alcoholic beverages for thousands of years. In *Alcohol: The Delightful Poison,* historian Alice Fleming explains the widespread use of this ancient drug:

> Alcohol has been intriguing and intoxicating human beings for at least seven thousand years. Nobody knows when, how, or by whom it was first discovered, but the chances are good that this happened by accident. Alcohol has turned up in different places at different times and in different forms [since before the start of recorded history]. There is scarcely an age or a culture in which it was not known.[3]

Clay tablets found in the ruins of ancient Babylon indicate its inhabitants brewed beer and drank it as part of their religious ceremonies as far back as 5000 B.C. Historians also know that the ancient Egyptians brewed beer, which they called *hek*. They did this by placing crumbled barley bread into jars and covering the bread with water to allow natural fermentation.

Wine making also began thousands of years ago. Wine, which is made from grapes, is mentioned in historical documents from Mesopotamia dating as far back as 3000 B.C. The most distinctive type of wine, champagne, was created in 1688 by Dom Pierre

This ancient model depicts Egyptians making bread and beer.

Perignon, a Roman Catholic monk in charge of the wine cellars at a Benedictine abbey in France. Champagne is named after the French province in which it was first made, and a famous brand of champagne bears Perignon's name.

In a sense, the techniques that brewers and wine makers developed over the centuries have simply been refinements of the natural process of fermentation. The beer and wine produced in this manner have comparatively low concentrations of alcohol, about 5 to 8 percent for beer and 12 percent for wine. That is because most strains of yeast, a catalyst in the chemical process of fermentation, cannot survive an alcohol concentration much above 14 percent. It was not until another alcohol-making process—distillation—was perfected that it was possible to make distilled spirits such as brandy and whiskey with higher alcohol concentrations.

The process of distillation is believed to have been first discovered during the eighth century in Arabia and then rediscovered almost five hundred years later during the thirteenth century by Arnauld de Villeneuve, a professor of medicine at the University of Montpelier in France. Distillation enables people to produce a drink with high alcohol concentration. These distilled alcoholic beverages are also referred to simply as "spirits" or "hard liquor." In distillation, a fermented beverage is heated until it vaporizes; the vapor is then cooled until it condenses again into a liquid, which has a much higher alcohol concentration. Distillation allowed de Villeneuve to produce pure alcohol, which he named *aqua vitae,* Latin for "water of life." This Latin term was translated as *usquebaugh* in Gaelic, a language spoken in Scotland, and eventually became the English word *whiskey.*

Religion and Alcohol

Alcohol has had many uses throughout history, including in religion. Alcohol's ability to intoxicate drinkers mystified ancient people so much that many of them came to believe that alcohol had been sent to them as a gift from the gods. The Greeks, for example, believed a mythological figure named Dionysus had originally taught people how to make wine. Even today alcohol has a central role in

*Pope John Paul II holds
aloft a chalice containing
wine during a Roman
Catholic mass.*

some religions. In Christianity wine serves as a symbol of the blood of Christ during communion, and in Judaism wine is drunk as part of the religious observance of the first day of Passover, the most important feast in the Jewish calendar.

In some cultures long ago, large quantities of alcohol were consumed during religious ceremonies in hopes of achieving closer communication with the gods. The Aztecs and many Native American tribes, for example, consumed alcohol and other intoxicating substances to accomplish this. In *Alcohol, Science and Society Revisited,* Dwight B. Heath states,

> In the early years of the fur trade in northeastern North America, it appears as if the Iroquois used brandy as they had previously used self-imposed partial starvation, as a means of assuring that a young man achieve the hallucinatory "vision" that would be the basis of his personal link with supernatural powers throughout the rest of his life.[4]

Some religions, however, reject the use of alcohol. The Muslim religion prohibits drinking. In the *Koran,* Islam's holy book, the prophet Mohammed advises adherents to abstain from alcohol: "The devil desires to sow dissensions and hatred among you through wine and games of chance, be obedient to God and the prophet, his apostle, and take heed to yourselves."[5]

Nonetheless, most cultures throughout history have considered alcoholic beverages a blessing, considering beer and other forms of alcohol important sources of food.

Alcohol as Food

Prior to the introduction of the potato, beer was second only to bread as the main source of nourishment for most central and northern Europeans. In 1551 historian Johann Brettschneier, referring not to hard-core drinkers but to average people, wrote: "Some subsist more upon this drink than they do on food. People of both sexes and every age, the hale and the infirm alike, require it."[6]

Although the only vitamin that beer has in significant amounts is riboflavin, beer and other alcoholic drinks provide a source of natural sugar. When an ounce of whiskey is broken down by digestion, it can release seventy-five calories of energy, about as much as four and a half teaspoons of sugar or a large slice of bread. Even though beer is not nutritious, it was considered a healthy food centuries ago because it imparted energy to people whose diet was often low in calories.

At a time when little was known about health or proper nutrition, alcohol also seemed to offer other benefits to those who drank it. For example, alcohol was prized because it was so good at masking pain associated with injury, illness, and arduous labor. Historian Mark Keller explains how alcohol seemed to aid workers in the past:

> At one time people thought that alcohol was especially helpful in doing hard work. They even supposed that heavy laborers could not work well without it. Some men labored so hard and long each day that they might not have been able to bear the pain and fatigue without the sedation of alcohol. As their labor was not skilled, the amounts they drank did not interfere noticeably with their efficiency.[7]

The sedative action of alcohol, which allows it to ease pain, was only one reason why people believed for centuries that alcohol was an indispensable part of their lives. In fact, in the past alcohol's most exalted status was as one of humankind's most ancient and effective medicines.

Healing Alcohol

When de Villeneuve discovered how to distill alcohol and named it "water of life," he argued, "This name is remarkably suitable, since it is really a water of immortality. It prolongs life, clears away [sickness], and maintains youth."[8] Two hundred years later, Hieronymous Brunschwig, a German doctor, referred to de Villeneuve's *aqua vitae* as "the mistress of all medicines" and claimed,

> It eases the diseases coming of cold, it comforts the heart, it heals all old and new sores on the head. It causes a good color in a person. It heals [baldness] and causes the hair well to grow, and kills lice and fleas. It cures lethargy. Cotton wet in the same and a little wrung out again and so put in the ears at night before going to bed . . . is of good [cure] against deafness.[9]

For many centuries, people in almost every society valued wine for its medicinal qualities, sometimes simply as the recommended liquid

---

Proof in Alcohol

Many of the terms related to alcohol are centuries old. One of these is *proof*, which refers to the alcohol content of a beverage. In *The Facts About Drinking: Coping with Alcohol Use, Abuse, and Alcoholism*, author Gail Gleason Milgram explains the archaic test from which this word evolved.

> The term "proof" is derived from a seventh century test in which an alcohol-containing liquid was mixed with gunpowder and set on fire. When the liquor was sufficiently free of water, the gunpowder would ignite and thereby establish the "proof" of alcohol [being present]. If the flame flared, there was too much alcohol; if it sputtered, there wasn't enough; and if it yielded a strong blue flame it was considered just right—about 57 percent alcohol by volume.

> (British and Canadian regulations still consider a concentration of 57.35 percent to be proof spirits.) Today, the degree of proof translates as twice the percentage of alcohol in the drink—that is, a 100 percent alcohol beverage would be 200 proof. [There is a] wide range of proof available in alcoholic beverages. One can buy wine that is 8 percent alcohol by volume, or 16 proof, and distilled spirits that range from approximately 25 percent to 45 percent alcohol or 50 to 90 proof. Although regular beers are usually around 4.5 percent alcohol, "light" beers and low-alcohol beers contain less.

Hippocrates, the Greek physician known as the father of medicine, considered wine an important medicine.

with which to consume other medical remedies. The Greek sage Hippocrates included wine in a list of important medicines, and Roman physicians endorsed it as a dressing for wounds, a fever fighter, and a restorative beverage. The *Talmud,* a Jewish book of wisdom, claims that "wine taken in moderation induces appetites and is beneficial to health. Wine is the greatest of medicines."[10]

Until the discovery of ether in 1846, alcohol was used to dull the pain of tooth extractions and surgery, and doctors often advised patients to drink it to kill any discomfort they were feeling from many other physical ailments. Alcohol was also considered an aid to preventing infection, especially after childbirth, and to calming victims who went into shock after an accident or traumatic experience. Doctors also prescribed alcohol for people who were unhappy or depressed because they believed alcohol would make their patients feel happier.

Physicians, in fact, believed so deeply in the healing powers of alcohol that they thought it could cure almost anything from shortness

*Alcoholic beverages are a
traditional part of many
social celebrations,
including weddings.*

of breath and hiccups to a bite from a poisonous snake. Doctors even
advised patients with sore knees and other inflamed joints to rub alcohol on the painful areas to relieve swelling or discomfort.

Although people in past centuries valued alcohol for its benefits as
a medicine and as a source of food, the main reason people have consumed alcohol has been its ability to make social gatherings more enjoyable. Drinking has thus become a traditional part of almost every
social occasion imaginable.

Social Drinking

Today alcohol is a welcome addition to most of life's personal and
public rites and rituals, something that was also true hundreds of
years ago. In his study of popular beliefs in sixteenth- and seventeenth-
century England, Keith Thomas writes,

[Alcohol] was built into the fabric of social life. It played a part in nearly every public and private ceremony, every commercial bargain, every craft ritual, every private occasion of mourning or rejoicing. As a Frenchman observed in 1672, there was no business which could be done in England without pots of beer.[11]

The English even gave a name to their inclusion of drinking into almost every social and business aspect of daily life. They termed such celebrations *cakes and ale,* and there were few occasions that failed to call for a round of drinks to make the event more festive and enjoyable. Beer, wine, and later distilled spirits such as brandy, gin, and whiskey became an established part of the way people commemorated special events in their lives, such as marriage or childbirth. Alcoholic beverages were also present when people celebrated the successful conclusion of business deals, honored special dates in their nation's history, or simply added to the enjoyment they got from getting together with members of their family or their friends.

Taverns

One of the drinking traditions the English brought to America was taverns—commercial establishments where people could drink alcoholic beverages and socialize with their friends. Many taverns played a role in the American Revolution as meeting places for patriots plotting to overthrow the British, and it was in a room above a tavern in Philadelphia where Thomas Jefferson wrote the Declaration of Independence. In *Drinking in America: A History,* Mark Lender and James Kirby Martin explain the importance of colonial taverns:

Taverns filled a variety of practical social needs. In many areas, they were the most convenient retail outlets for liquor—and often the only place where travelers could find food and lodging. They provided all localities with a forum for social intercourse, which often included political, religious, or other gatherings. Before and during the Revolution, for example, inns were favorite places for political discussions, and they served as rallying points for the militia and as recruiting stations for the Continental army. Innkeepers ideally reflected the high public status accorded their establishments, and in reality they often did. Publicans [tavern owners] were commonly among a town's most prominent citizens and not infrequently were deacons [in their church]. While some taverns were only rude structures with plank bars—there were a lot of these in port towns like New York, Philadelphia, and Charleston and on the sparsely settled frontier—others were well-appointed, pleasant places to spend time. The taverns were a vital early American institution—an institution highly regarded by most colonials and attended as faithfully as many churches.

When the English began to settle the New World, they brought their drinking traditions with them, and that meant that early Americans also drank a lot—per capita alcohol consumption in colonial America was more than twice what it is today. Historian Don Cahalan explains that beer, wine, and other beverages played an important role in early American society:

> No other element seemed capable of satisfying so many human needs. It [alcohol] contributed to the success of any festive occasion and [eased] those in sorrow and distress. It gave courage to the soldier, endurance to the traveler, foresight to the statesman, and inspiration to the preacher. It sustained the sailor and plowman, the trader and trapper. By it were lighted the fires of revelry and of devotion. Few doubted that it was a great boon to mankind. [12]

People also drank just to have a good time, and psychologist Abraham Myerston writes that the relaxing, social aspect of alcohol is still its most important use in daily life today:

Early American taverns were not only places to drink but establishments where people gathered to eat and be social.

> There are times when, and places where, that chemical physiological com-
> pound known as man needs chemicals to alter his reactions. Alcohol is a sort
> of chemotherapy for undue stress. It releases exuberance, good fellowship,
> and friendliness, all of which are exceedingly valuable to man. [13]

There is, however, an inherent danger to social drinking, and that
is that some drinkers will consume so much alcohol that they create
problems for themselves and the rest of society. Excessive drinking by
some people has been a problem for as long as alcohol has been
around, but during the eighteenth century an epidemic of ruinous alcohol consumption swept through England. This first widespread
breakdown of social drinking became known as "gin fever."

Gin Fever

During the 1700s the drinking preference of hundreds of thousands
of English people suddenly and dramatically changed from beer and
ale to gin, a generic name at the time for gin, brandy, rum and other
distilled spirits, which had much higher percentages of alcohol. Distilled spirits had been available in Europe since the Middle Ages, but
up until the sixteenth century they had been expensive and were
taken mainly for medical reasons.

The popularity of these liquors soared among the poor when new
manufacturing methods enabled distillers to produce them more
cheaply than beer or ale. In *Tastes of Paradise: A Social History of
Spices, Stimulants, and Intoxicants,* Wolfgang Schivelbusch explains
that the large-scale switch to drinking distilled spirits was disastrous:

> Liquor dealt a death blow to traditional drinking, which had been based on
> wine and beer. Whereas beer and wine are drunk slowly in long sips, and the
> inebriation process is gradual, liquor is *tossed off,* and intoxication is more or
> less instantaneous. Liquor thus represents a process of *acceleration* of intoxica-
> tion. Gin struck the typically beer-drinking English populace like a thunder-
> bolt. Traditional drinking patterns could not cope with this highly
> concentrated inebriant. Drinking and intoxication totally lost their characteris-
> tic role of establishing social bonds or connections. Inebriation [mild drunk-
> enness] gave way to alcoholic stupor. [14]

The new style of drinking crippled English society and by the mid-
1700s widespread drunkenness was common, especially in major
cities. Excessive liquor consumption was a contributing factor to a

British artist William Hogarth depicts the evil effects of drinking in his engraving, "Gin Lane." Many English cities during this period were populated with thousands of drunken men and women.

huge increase in robberies, murders, and brawls; thousands of men and women died from overdrinking and thousands more drank so much they were unable to work. This is how noted eighteenth-century author Henry Fielding described this disastrous national drinking spree:

A new kind of drunkenness, unknown to our ancestors, is lately sprung up amongst us, and which, if not put a stop to, will infallibly destroy a great part of the inferior people. The drunkenness I here intend is that acquired by the strongest intoxicating liquors and particularly by that poison called Gin which I have reason to think is the principal sustenance (if it may be so called) of more than a hundred thousand people in this metropolis [London].[15]

This ruinous drinking began to decrease during the second half of the eighteenth century after the English government acted to curb the sale of distilled spirits. Starting with the Gin Act in 1736, Parliament levied increasingly higher taxes on liquor, making it too expensive for most people to drink in large quantities. The act also created rigid regulations governing its sale, such as limiting the hours that taverns could do business. Such laws led most people to resume drinking more beer and ale than liquor, which helped reduce the problems.

Evil and Good

Alcohol has always been a mixed blessing for humankind, able to create misery as well as provide enjoyment for those who use it. In 1673

Gin Lane and Beer Street

William Hogarth, one of England's most famous eighteenth-century artists, is best known for engravings that commented satirically on social ills. One of his most famous works is *Gin Lane,* a frightening rendering of the epidemic of drunkenness caused by gin and other distilled spirits. By comparison, the companion piece *Beer Street* shows a scene of peace and prosperity. Hogarth, like many others of his era, believed it was healthy to drink beer and ale but thought consuming distilled spirits was bad for people. In *Tastes of Paradise: A Social History of Spices, Stimulants, and Intoxicants,* Wolfgang Schivelbusch comments on these diverse attitudes toward alcohol.

This famous engraving depicting the world's ruin through liquor is a comment upon the so-called epidemic of the eighteenth century. While Gin Lane offers an image of destruction—collapsing houses, a dehumanized mother who drops her child, people assaulting one another, suicides, and only the pawnbroker's shop thriving—in its counterimage, Beer Street, peace, contentedness, and industriousness prevail. This contrast of beer and hard liquor survived into nineteenth- and twentieth-century discussions [of social problems]. [Beer] was viewed as a guarantee of happiness, contentment, health. The world of beer was all right; with liquor the world came apart at the seams.

*Increase Mather, a famous
religious leader in early
colonial America, believed
the Devil caused heavy
drinking.*

Increase Mather, a noted clergyman and early president of Harvard College, commented on the twin nature of alcohol in *Wo to Drunkards:* "Drink is in itself a good creature of God, and to be received with thankfulness, but the abuse of drink is from Satan."[16]

Scientists today know that it is not evil spirits that cause problems when people drink. They are also learning more every day about how alcohol works its chemical magic to intoxicate people and, sometimes, to addict them.

Chapter 2

Alcohol's Effect on the Body

Perhaps because beer, wine, and other alcoholic beverages are so common in everyday life, most people do not think of alcohol as a drug. But alcohol is a drug, a powerful central nervous system depressant that is generally classified with similar drugs such as barbiturates, minor tranquilizers, and general anesthetics. As a depressant, alcohol depresses, or slows down, the operation of the central nervous system, which includes the brain and the spinal cord.

The depressed performance of the central nervous system caused by alcohol consumption creates the slurred speech, impaired physical coordination, and other physical signs that indicate a person has been drinking. But in *Under the Influence: A Guide to the Myths and Realities of Alcoholism*, authors James R. Milam and Katherine Ketcham explain that this drug is complex in the variety of ways it can affect the human body: "Alcohol is an infinitely confusing substance. In small amounts it is an exhilarating stimulant. In larger amounts it acts as a sedative and as a toxin, or poisonous, agent."[17]

Thus, when people first begin drinking, they usually feel happy and more energetic. As they consume more and more alcohol, however, the drug's depressive effects begin to emerge, creating the behavior associated with being intoxicated. Finally, if a person consumes

*Friends toast each other before a meal. Eating decreases the speed with
which alcohol is absorbed into the bloodstream.*

enough alcohol at one time, this drug can be deadly. And all of these
complex reactions to alcohol begin in one place—the brain.

Alcohol and the Brain

Alcohol is easily and quickly absorbed into the body. This process begins before the drinker even swallows a sip of beer or wine because 5
to 10 percent of alcohol is transferred to the bloodstream directly
through the lining of the mouth. The beverage then passes through
the stomach and small intestine, where a high concentration of small
blood vessels speeds absorption into the bloodstream. As alcohol
moves into the bloodstream, it spreads throughout the body. However, its effect on the brain is almost immediate. There are two reasons for this: a substantial portion of the blood that the heart pumps
goes directly to the brain, and the brain's fatty material readily and
easily absorbs alcohol.

People have understood for thousands of years that drinking beer,
wine, and liquor makes them intoxicated, but it was not until the last
two decades of the twentieth century that scientists discovered how

alcohol actually does this. As late as 1974 the National Institutes of Health (NIH) issued a report saying, "No one knows how alcohol intoxicates [people]."[18] But by 2000, in its *Tenth Special Report to the U.S. Congress on Alcohol and Health*, researchers for the NIH and its National Institute on Alcohol Abuse and Alcoholism (NIAAA) finally had the answer: "The changes in behavior seen soon after consumption of alcohol—as well as the euphoria and anxiety reductions seen with alcohol—all result from alcohol's actions on the brain."[19]

The brain and spinal cord make up the central nervous system, which controls physical behavior like walking as well as involuntary actions necessary for life, such as breathing and the beating of the heart. The central nervous system runs along the spinal cord and branches out into every part of the body. The brain is in continuous

---

How Blood Alcohol Levels Rise

How intoxicated people become when they drink depends on how fast their liver can process alcohol. A normal, healthy liver can break down and eliminate 0.5 ounces of pure alcohol from the bloodstream each hour, which is the equivalent of 12 ounces of beer, 5 ounces of table wine, or 1.5 ounces of 80-proof distilled spirits. When people drink more than those amounts in an hour, their blood alcohol levels (BALs) will go up; if the levels rise high enough, they will become drunk. The following is an example of how this happens, taken from *Beyond the Influence: Understanding and Defeating Alcoholism.*

> It's a Sunday evening in Denver, the Broncos have just won the Super Bowl, and Joe is in a party mood. Around 8 P.M. he joins some friends at a local tavern, and in the next four hours he downs twelve beers and four shots of 80-proof tequila. In all the excitement, Joe, who weighs 165 pounds, forgets to eat dinner, munching on pretzels and potato chips instead. By midnight, when Joe falls into bed, his liver has burned up 2 ounces of pure alcohol (about four beers). By 6:00 A.M., when he wakes up, his liver has eliminated an additional 3 ounces (six more beers). On his way to work at 7:00 A.M., Joe still has approximately 2 ounces of pure alcohol circulating around in his bloodstream (the remaining beers and 4 ounces of tequila). Seven hours after Joe stopped drinking, he is still legally drunk. Unfortunately for Joe, there's nothing he can do to nudge his liver along and accelerate the metabolic process. Coffee, cold showers, fruit juice, and exercise are all basically useless, for the fact remains that if you drink more than your liver can process at one time, your [BAL] will rise. If you keep drinking, you'll get drunk. And the more you drink, the drunker you'll get.

direct communication with all of these parts, sending messages through this system to control its actions. These directives, which are in effect commands to various muscles and parts of the body, pass between individual cells via what are called neurotransmitters.

The latest research on drinking shows that alcohol interferes with this flow of commands from the brain at the level of the neurotransmitters, and that this disruption of communication from the brain is the major change that causes intoxication. Thus, intoxication is caused by alcohol working directly on the brain to dull or hamper the way it works.

Intoxication is a gradual process; it does not occur after a person has consumed one drink but several. This is because alcohol in the bloodstream has to build to sufficient levels to start affecting how the brain operates.

Alcohol Levels

Alcohol is processed in the body through a series of chemical reactions. These reactions—called metabolism—break down food and other ingested substances to simple compounds the body can use. The liver is the organ that does the bulk of this work. It metabolizes alcohol, re-

The Amount of Alcohol in One Drink

 12 ounces of beer (5% alcohol)

 5 ounces of wine (12% alcohol)

 1.5 ounces of liquor (40% alcohol)

Each of the three types of alcohol listed above has about the same amount of ethyl alcohol—**.5 ounces**.

A police officer gives a driver a sobriety test. Alcohol seriously impairs physical coordination, such as a person's ability to touch his or her nose.

moving it from the bloodstream at a constant rate of one standard drink per hour. A standard drink is defined as 12 ounces of beer, 5 ounces of wine, or 1.5 ounces of 80-proof distilled spirits, all of which contain .5 ounces of alcohol. Because the human body can only process alcohol at that fixed rate of one drink per hour, people who consume more than one drink per hour will gradually increase the alcohol levels in their blood. The result of this is that they will become intoxicated.

The body's blood alcohol concentration (BAC), also known as blood alcohol level (BAL), is the medically recognized method for calculating how much someone has had to drink. The BAC is the amount of alcohol in the blood measured in percentages; a BAC of 0.10 percent, for example, means that a person's bloodstream has one part alcohol per one thousand parts of blood.

As alcohol levels rise, intoxication begins. The effects of intoxication are many and varied, and they continually change as people keep drinking.

Intoxication

The types of behavior that begin occurring soon after people start drinking alcohol are collectively referred to as intoxication. This state includes impaired physical coordination and mental performance as well as changes in a person's emotions, including a feeling of relaxation and a lessening of fear or anxiety over personal problems. Although for most people these initial sensations are usually pleasant, the effects of alcohol intensify as drinkers consume more alcohol. This leads to difficulty in how a person reacts and responds physically, mentally, and emotionally to what is happening around him or her.

The way alcohol affects people is complex, however, and the effects it creates change as people drink more and more. Although alcohol is a depressant, it acts more like a stimulant when people first take a drink. Moderate doses of alcohol increase blood flow, accelerate the heart rate, and stimulate brain cells to speed the transmission of nerve impulses. In *Beyond the Influence: Understanding and Defeating Alcoholism*, Katherine Ketcham and William F. Asbury explain that these physiological changes in turn create a feeling of emotional well-being, which is the main reason that people enjoy drinking:

> We turn to alcohol for relaxation and stress reduction, and the drug delivers almost immediately by making us feel happy, energetic, and at peace with ourselves. These pleasurable, tension-relieving sensations are due to alcohol's stimulating effects on the body, particularly the brain and the heart.[20]

In an average person, one standard drink will produce a light feeling of pleasantness or exhilaration. People who consume two glasses of wine or bottles of beer will tend to have a heightened feeling of relaxation coupled with a decrease in fine motor skills, and those who have three drinks will begin to have slower physical reaction times, decreased muscular control, and slurred speech. Even at this stage, many people will still be able to function almost normally physically and mentally, although some drinkers, especially those who do not drink often, may begin to experience some problems.

However, the more people drink the more intoxicated they will become. And as the level of alcohol in their system rises, alcohol will begin creating new and quite different physical and mental reactions.

Drunkenness

Because the initial sensations of intoxication are so enjoyable, most people continue drinking alcohol in an attempt to heighten them.

Blood Alcohol Level and Intoxication

The amount of alcohol in a person's bloodstream is referred to as blood alcohol level (BAL) or blood alcohol concentration (BAC). It is recorded in milligrams of alcohol per 100 milliliters of blood; a BAC of 0.10 means that 1/10 of 1 percent of total blood content is alcohol. A reading of 0.10 percent is considered legal proof that a person is drunk in most states. The following are some examples of the observable effects of certain BALs on occasional social drinkers (because of their higher tolerance, an alcoholic or problem drinker must have BALs several times higher before alcohol will create the same effects in them).

At 0.03 to 0.05 percent, a flushed face, feeling of euphoria, and increased social confidence; at 0.50 to 0.15 percent, disturbed thinking and coordination, reduced self-control, irresponsible talk and behavior; at 0.15 to 0.25 percent, confused thinking, unsteady gait, slurred speech; at 0.25 to 0.40 percent, extreme confusion and disorientation, difficulty remaining upright, drowsiness, risk of falling into a coma (a state of deep unconsciousness from which the person cannot be aroused); 0.40 to 0.50 percent, risk of death due to cessation of breathing (although habitual drinkers may survive even such high levels).

Blood Alcohol Concentration Within One Hour

number of drinks

weight in pounds	1	2	3	4	5	
100	.04	.09	.15	.20	.25	**0 to .04** Not legally under the influence. Impairment possible.
120	.03	.08	.12	.16	.21	
140	.02	.06	.10	.14	.18	**.05 to .09** State laws regarding BAC legal limits vary. Mental and physical impairment noticeable.
160	.02	.05	.09	.12	.15	
180	.02	.05	.08	.10	.13	**.10 and above** Presumed intoxicated in all 50 states.
200	.01	.04	.07	.09	.12	

Figures are rounded to nearest .01. BACs shown are approximate, since they can be affected by factors other than weight.

The problem is that as people consume more alcohol, it begins to act like the type of drug it really is—a depressant—and it has a sedative effect. Rising levels of alcohol in a person's bloodstream begin to slow nerve and brain activity and at very high levels will make a person unconscious as surely as a sleeping pill.

Consuming large quantities of alcohol can cause unconsciousness.

When people are in this heightened stage of intoxication, they are commonly said to be drunk. It is alcohol's depressant power that creates the physical changes most people associate with someone who is drunk, such as inarticulate or slurred speech, out-of-focus eyes, and jerky, out-of-synch physical movements, including a staggering walk. These effects are opposite from those produced initially by small doses of alcohol, when the drug had a mildly stimulating effect on the drinker.

The severity of intoxication or drunkenness is linked directly to how much alcohol a person has in his or her bloodstream. As blood alcohol concentrations continue to increase, drinkers will have more and more trouble performing everyday tasks such as walking and talking, and even their vision will eventually become blurred.

At BACs higher than 0.30 percent, the drinker will be in a semi-stupor and can pass out, falling asleep for a short time or even several hours. When BACs reach 0.50 percent, a person can fall into a deep coma and will be in danger of dying. At even higher levels, alcohol works as a poison. It can kill by depressing the intoxicated person's brain activity so much that the drinker will stop breathing. This form of death is known as "alcohol poisoning."

The physical effects of alcohol are the most noticeable and the easiest to understand. However, the changes that take place in a drinker's mental and emotional states are just as dramatic.

Intoxicated Behavior

Just as alcohol can impair a drinker's physical behavior, it can also diminish the ability to reason and think clearly. Drinkers who become intoxicated discover that it becomes harder to remember things, to concentrate on what they are doing or saying, to understand what is happening to them and to others around them, and to make judgments concerning situations in which they are involved. An intoxicated person's ability to think and reason can become as garbled and disjointed as his or her attempts to speak. Harry Milt, author of *Alcoholism, Its Causes and Cure: A New Handbook*, explains that this impairment is one that sneaks up on people as they keep drinking:

> With the first drink or two an illusion may be created of clarity of mind and thought [but] as the alcohol continues to bathe the brain, consciousness becomes blurred, thinking is slowed down, the content of thought is [reduced], memory is blurred. Concepts are poorly formulated, reasoning is foggy, judgment is blunted. [21]

Talking to someone who is intoxicated often seems like conversing with a child. People who are drunk often fail to understand what someone is telling them, keep interrupting to say something unrelated to what the other person is saying, and usually have trouble listening

How Alcohol Acts on the Brain

Scientists now understand that people become intoxicated by the way alcohol affects their brain's ability to control the body. This process is very complex, but in its *Tenth Special Report to the U.S. Congress on Alcohol and Health,* which summarizes the latest research on alcohol and how it affects people, the NIH and NIAAA provide a simplified explanation of how this happens.

The brain communicates through neurons, nerve cells that are specialized to receive and rapidly conduct chemical and electrical signals. Electrical signals help fulfill the neuron's major role—to communicate information quickly to the rest of the body so that the brain can carry out its many functions. Neurotransmitters in each cell enable these signals to travel from the brain to all parts of the body. The Tenth Special Report states, "Alcohol appears to affect the function of several neurotransmitters by altering the communication mechanism between neurons. A large body of evidence suggests that this effect of alcohol on transmission [of signals from the brain] is the major change in the brain that gives rise to intoxication." In simple terms, this means that alcohol works on the cellular level to disrupt communication from the brain, resulting in the physical, mental, and emotional behaviors associated with intoxication.

for very long because they are easily distracted. Drunk people act very much as if their intelligence has been diminished—which it is, temporarily—because their brains are not functioning correctly.

In addition to the problems intoxicated drinkers have in knowing and understanding what is going on around them intellectually, changes also take place in their emotional state. Most people feel happy when they have their first few drinks. As they drink more and more, however, their emotions change, often in a volatile way as they experience radical swings between moods as varied as joy, sadness, happiness, and anger. Increased consumption can also bring out negative personality characteristics such as aggressiveness and cruelty.

One of the main effects of alcohol, as well as one of its most damaging, is to lessen people's inhibitions, making it easier for them to surrender to negative impulses or emotions they normally would resist. Sociologist Sherri Cavan writes that alcohol makes drinkers feel that "the constraint and respect the social world ordinarily requires [of their behavior] is no longer demanded [of them]."[22] For example, when intoxicated drinkers become angry at someone, they often lash out physically at that person even though they would not do so if they were sober.

As with the physical effects of intoxication, the mental and emotional changes that take place continue to intensify as people consume more alcohol. The severity of this intoxication can be correlated directly to the drinker's blood alcohol levels; the higher the BAC, the drunker the person will be.

However, the degree of intoxication from drinking the same amount of alcohol will vary among individuals and even in the same individual at different times. That is because several important factors influence how rapidly alcohol will make someone intoxicated.

People who are drunk have trouble controlling emotions such as anger, causing some drinkers to behave violently.

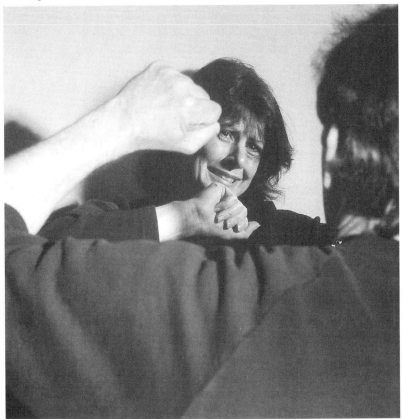

Factors in Becoming Intoxicated

Because of the way alcohol circulates in the body, a person's size plays an important part in determining how quickly alcohol will affect him or her and how drunk that person will become. A person weighing 220 pounds, for instance, will not become as intoxicated by the same number of drinks as a person weighing 120 pounds. Because the blood supply is correspondingly bigger, a similar amount of alcohol will be more diluted in the larger person's body. Another consideration is whether the drinker has eaten lately. The presence of food in a person's stomach will slow down how quickly alcohol is absorbed into the bloodstream.

There are also individual variances in the speed with which people metabolize alcohol because of their own unique body chemistry. The gender of the drinker makes a difference because women usually absorb and metabolize alcohol more quickly than men, which means they will have higher BACs after consuming the same amount of alcohol.

A key factor is whether the person having a drink is a regular drinker. Dr. Gail Gleason Milgram explains that experience with alcohol plays a part in how intoxicated people will become by consuming the same amount of alcohol:

> Someone drinking a glass of wine [for the first time] may experience light-headedness but will probably not experience that effect on subsequent occasions. However, most individuals who drink know what to expect from various amounts of alcohol because of their prior experience with drinking.[23]

The reason for this is that when people drink on a regular basis, their bodies build up a physical tolerance to alcohol that helps them stay sober. Regular drinkers also become so accustomed to what alcohol does to their bodies that they can better cope with the changes alcohol causes.

Health Dangers

Although alcohol's effects are powerful, there are not many immediate health risks from occasional drinking. For those who do drink too much, the most common health problem is a hangover, the symptoms of which include headaches, nausea, and other bodily discomfort. A hangover can last for hours or even days depending on how much the person drank.

This nineteenth-century cartoon depicts the physical price people pay for drinking too much.

Occasional drinkers must also be careful to make sure they are not taking any medication that could interact with the alcohol they are consuming. In some cases, alcohol can react with prescription drugs to make a person very ill.

A Dangerous Drug

Although there are not many health risks for those who drink moderately once in a while, alcohol in large amounts is both powerful and potentially dangerous. Many serious health consequences exist for people who drink a lot over a long period, including liver and brain damage.

Alcohol is also highly addictive, and when a person becomes hooked on drinking, this drug can destroy his or her life. In *The Facts About Drugs and Alcohol,* Dr. Mark S. Gold explains just how dangerous this drug can be. "Alcohol," he writes," is the most destructive drug known to mankind . . . without a doubt, the world's most abused substance."[24]

Chapter 3

Alcohol Abuse and Addiction

The National Institute on Alcohol Abuse and Alcoholism (NIAAA), a federal agency that researches and educates the public about alcohol use, defines moderate alcohol consumption as up to two standard drinks per day for men and one for women and older people, amounts that are not considered physically harmful. Addiction expert Margaret O. Hyde explains that the vast majority of people who drink are able to limit their alcohol intake to these safe levels:

> For most people, alcohol is not addictive and may never be a problem. In moderate amounts, the indirect effect of alcohol on the body is usually one of stimulation that produces a mood of emotional freedom. Most people who drink do so in a responsible manner by carefully choosing the time, place, and amount. [25]

But some people are unable to limit or control their drinking. Once they start drinking they seemingly cannot stop and will continue downing bottles of beer and shots of liquor long after other people have realized it is prudent to quit. It is estimated that 15 million adults (15 percent of the drinkers in the United States) regularly consume more than the recommended daily amount and that just 10 percent of drinkers account for 50 percent of the alcohol drunk in the nation each year. Their drinking has become abnormal, a condition that has devastating consequences for them and for everyone who comes in contact with them.

Alcoholic Drinking

The word *alcoholic* and its companion word, *alcoholism*, were coined in 1848 by Magnus Huss, a Swedish scientist. Prior to that time, the condition was referred to as chronic or continual drunkenness, and the person who suffered from the condition was known as a drunkard. In his landmark 1960 book *The Disease Concept of Alcoholism*, Dr. E. M. Jellinek, who did more than anyone else to make the medical establishment recognize alcoholism as a disease, provided a simple definition for this kind of destructive drinking: "Alcoholism is any use of alcoholic beverages that causes any damage to the individual or society or both."[26] Jellinek made his explanation of this disease so simple and broad that everyone could understand it and accept it.

Alcohol Abuse and Dependence

Today medical experts group alcoholism with addictions to other drugs, such as cocaine and heroin, under the overall category of *substance dependence*, a term for addiction to any drug. Medical experts also make a distinction between *alcohol abuse* and the latter term being considered synonymous with *alcoholism*. The National Institute on Alcohol Abuse and Alcoholism (NIAAA) defines alcohol abuse as a pattern of continued alcohol use that causes recurring problems such as

> failure to fulfill major work, school, or home responsibilities; drinking in situations that are physically dangerous, such as while driving a car or operating machinery; recurring alcohol-related legal problems, such as being arrested for driving under the influence of alcohol or for physically hurting someone while drunk; continuing drinking while having ongoing relationship problems that are caused or worsened by the effects of alcohol.

Alcohol dependence, more commonly known as alcoholism, is a more serious level of alcohol use, one in which people are considered addicted. Although the NIAAA notes that alcoholics experience the same lifestyle problems it outlined for alcohol abuse, its definition of alcohol dependence focuses on four physical and emotional changes that have taken place in the drinker. They are craving, which is a strong need or compulsion to drink; loss of control, the frequent inability to stop drinking once the person has begun; physical dependence, the occurrence of withdrawal symptoms such as nausea, sweating, and anxiety when alcohol use ends after a period of heavy drinking; and tolerance, the need to consume increasing amounts of alcohol to become intoxicated.

This nineteenth-century print shows a wife and her daughter trying to make her husband leave a tavern.

In the decades since Jellinek defined alcoholism, medical experts have refined his original concept. Alcoholism is now considered an addiction, one that is potentially as destructive to the individual as an addiction to illegal drugs such as cocaine or heroin. The medical field has also created new terminology for heavy drinkers that can be used in place of *alcoholic*. Generally, anyone who drinks too much on a consistent basis can be considered a *problem drinker*. Medical experts also differentiate between someone who *abuses alcohol* and someone who suffers from *alcohol dependence;* the latter term is considered synonymous with being addicted to alcohol.

Whatever term is used to refer to them, the number of people who suffer severe drinking problems is actually quite small. In 2001 the NIAAA estimated that 1 in every 13 adults, nearly 14 million people or 7.4 percent of the nation's population, abused alcohol or was alcohol dependent, and several million more people consumed so much alcohol that they were at risk of having such problems in the future.

For thousands of years, the question of why some people are unable to control their drinking has bewildered the world's greatest thinkers. In recent decades, however, research has uncovered several important risk factors that can lead people into destructive drinking patterns. These include family history, societal values, and individual psychological makeup.

The most decisive factor in whether someone will have trouble with alcohol is his or her genetic makeup. How a person responds to alcohol is directly related to physiological characteristics passed from parents to children.

Genetics

Centuries before Austrian botanist Gregor Mendel laid the mathematical framework for the science of genetics in 1866, many people already believed that alcoholism ran in families. They could easily see that sons and daughters of heavy drinkers all too often drank too

Genetics and Alcoholism

Scientists are currently trying to understand how a person's genetic makeup affects their health, such as whether they will be susceptible to heart disease or cancer. This genetic investigation also includes research into why some people are more susceptible than others to having problems controlling their drinking. Research has already proven that a person's genetic makeup can increase his or her risk of having drinking problems, including studies on twins separated at birth who both grew up to become alcoholics. Genetic study of alcoholism now centers on finding which genes influence how a person reacts to alcohol. However, the *Tenth Special Report to the U.S. Congress on Alcohol and Health*, which was issued in 2000, explains that finding the genetic key to this disease will take time.

Research has not yet pinpointed specific genes that "predispose" a person to alcohol abuse or dependence. Once researchers know the genes, they will have potent targets for their exploration of the biochemical processes that underlie the response to alcohol. Identifying all the genes involved is a project of enormous magnitude and difficulty, because of the size of the human [genetic code] and the complexity of the behaviors involved in drinking.

much themselves. Benjamin Rush, a doctor and signer of the Declaration of Independence, noted in his 1784 book *An Inquiry into the Effect of Ardent Spirits upon the Human Body and Mind* that "drunkenness resembles certain hereditary, family, and contagious diseases." [27]

The only evidence Rush had to support his theory was the general observations he could make on the behavior of people around him. As researchers learned more about genetics during the twentieth century and began to understand the role that genes play in human development, they were able to determine through scientific studies what Rush had only been able to understand intuitively. In a report to Congress in 2000, the NIAAA stated, "Today we know that approximately 50 to 60 percent of the risk for developing alcoholism is genetic." [28]

Research has shown that if one biological parent is an alcoholic, the likelihood of a child becoming dependent on alcohol is nearly three times greater; when both parents are alcoholic, the risk in-

Alcoholism in Families

Researchers believe that children who grow up in an alcoholic family have a much greater risk of developing problems with alcohol. The article "Why Do Some People Drink Too Much?" in the January 2000 issue of *Alcohol Research and Health,* discusses some of the reasons why alcoholism runs in families.

One of the main points the article makes is that alcoholic mothers and fathers are usually poor parents. They create a home atmosphere which is tense and at times frightening because of their angry, sometimes bizarre behavior while they are drinking drunk. Likewise, most alcoholic parents fail to support their children emotionally, do not know how to make them feel loved, and usually fail to offer their children any guidance in dealing with their own problems.

A family history of alcoholism is a well-established risk factor for the development of alcoholism. Some of the parenting deficits in alcoholic families are associated with the development of early conduct problems and early onset of alcohol use, which itself is a risk factor for later problems with alcohol use. Children of these families may not learn emotional and behavioral self-regulation and may lack social skills.

creases almost five times. People's genetic makeup determines not only how tall they will grow or what color their eyes and hair will be, but how their own unique body chemistry will react to various foods and liquids they consume, including alcohol. Children born to alcoholics often inherit genes that make it easier for them to drink a lot without getting sick or make alcohol more enjoyable for them than other people. Their genetic makeup, in effect, makes them vulnerable to becoming addicted because they are more likely to drink a lot.

However, some genetic traits can reduce the risk of a person becoming an alcoholic. Marc Schuckit, a psychiatrist and addiction specialist at the University of California at San Diego School of Medicine, states that many Asians have body chemistries that respond adversely to alcohol:

> Let's say that you're one of the 50 percent of Asian individuals—Japanese, Chinese, or Koreans—who flush when they drink. This means your face turns red and your heart beats fast and hard. It's not pleasant. In its extreme form, that negative reaction protects you from developing alcoholism quite well and in its modest form, which is found in 40 percent of Asian men and women, it decreases your risk a tad. [29]

Thus, a person's genetic makeup can, in many ways, determine whether it will be easy or difficult for them to drink alcohol. Most of this gene research today centers on what happens when this drug reaches the brain.

A Brain Disease

During the last two decades of the twentieth century, scientists learned that intoxication is caused by how alcohol affects the brain. Similar studies have shown that alcohol dependence can be linked to how alcohol reacts with the brain and how it can change the brain through long-term exposure. "The fact is," explains Dr. Alan I. Leshner, director of the National Institute of Drug Abuse (NIDA), "[alcohol] addiction is a brain disease."[30]

The first way that the brain influences whether a person will have trouble controlling his or her drinking is how it reacts to alcohol. When addictive substances such as alcohol reach the brain, they cause the release of dopamine, a chemical that produces sensations of pleasure. Generally, people who become addicted to alcohol experience intense pleasure the first time they drink. Gloria, an alcoholic, remembers that when she drank for the first time at age fifteen, "it really made me feel good. For the first time, I really felt *all right*."[31]

The pleasurable sensation Gloria experienced was caused by the release of dopamine. One theory that researchers are investigating is whether the brains of alcoholics like Gloria respond to alcohol by releasing more dopamine than those of other people, thus heightening their enjoyment and making it more likely they will drink again. But dopamine also plays another important role in addicting people to alcohol.

Chronic drinkers consume enormous amounts of alcohol over a long period. The large quantities of alcohol can lead to addiction by changing the way the brain functions. One alteration that occurs over time in heavy alcohol users is that their brains release increasingly smaller amounts of dopamine, reducing the pleasurable sensations they had been getting from drinking. "People take drugs initially," Leshner explains, "because they like what they do to their brains. But after someone's been using a drug for a long time, and this is true for all addictive substances, they actually go into a state where dopamine is lowered."[32]

The result of lowered dopamine levels is that people will drink more so they can experience the same level of pleasure that they previously had. Dr. Steven Hyman, director of the National Institute of Mental Health (NIMH), explains why this happens:

> They [drugs] tap right into a pleasure/reward circuit that we have in our brains, whose job it is to say something like, "Yes, that was good. Let's do it again and let's remember exactly how we did it." People will take these drugs again and again and again [to get that former feeling back].[33]

The way a person's brain responds to alcohol is greatly influenced by genetic makeup. Genetic makeup is not the only risk factor, however. Gene researchers like Dr. John Crabbe, director of the Portland Alcohol Research Center at Oregon University, stress the need to study other risk factors for this complex disease: "The key to the future is in understanding the interactions between genes and the environment."[34] By environment, Crabbe means families and society—two more key factors that influence how a person responds to alcohol when he or she begins drinking.

Habitual drinking lowers dopamine levels, subsequently requiring a higher intake of alcohol to achieve similar sensations of pleasure.

Parental Influence

David J. Hanson, a sociology professor with the State University of New York at Potsdam, believes that a mother and father have more power than anyone else to shape their children's beliefs, attitudes, and behaviors toward alcohol: "Parents are much more influential than they generally realize."[35] In support of his statement, Hanson cites a poll in the August 1996 issue of the Roper Youth Report. When asked what or who could sway their decisions about drinking, 62 percent of American youths aged twelve to seventeen identified their parents as the leading influence.

The strong role parents play in shaping their children's attitudes toward drinking is another reason—in addition to their genetic inheritance—that children of alcoholics are likely to struggle with alcohol. Although some young people who grow up in alcoholic homes vow never to follow the example set by their parents, studies show that many young people repeat the behaviors they see in their own homes. They may come to believe that consuming a great deal of alcohol and even getting drunk every day is a normal way to live and that alcohol is an important—even necessary—part of any family or social occasion. Those beliefs make it as easy for them to be trapped by alcohol as were their parents. Conversely, children whose parents abstain or drink moderately are more likely to follow that example when they become adults.

Reprinted with permission from Ed Gamble.

Children of Alcoholics

Children of alcoholics can find life at home very confusing. Alcoholic parents can be unpredictable and home life unsettling. In her book *Adult Children of Alcoholics,* Janet Geringer Woititz discusses how it feels to grow up with alcoholic parents.

> The only thing you were sure of was that you never knew what you would find, or what was going to happen. And somehow, no matter how many times things went awry, as soon as you walked in the door, you were never prepared. If your father was the alcoholic, sometimes he was loving and warm, he was everything you wanted a father to be: caring, interested, involved, promising all the things that a child wants. And you knew he loved you. But other times he wasn't that way. Those were the times he was drunk. When he didn't come home at all, you worried and waited. At home, he passed out, got into big fights with your mother. Sometimes you got in the middle, trying to keep the peace. Never knowing what was going to happen you always felt somewhat desperate. You probably had fantasies about leaving home, about running away, about having it over with, about your alcoholic parent becoming sober and life being fine and beautiful. You began to live in a fairy-tale world with fantasy and in dreams. You lived a lot on hope, because you didn't want to believe what was happening. You knew that you couldn't talk about it with your friends or adults outside your family, because you believed you had to keep these feelings to yourself, you learned to keep most of your other feelings to yourself. You couldn't let the rest of the world know what was going on in your home. Who would believe you, anyway?

Research has also found that an early introduction to alcohol increases a person's risk of having drinking problems. Studies show that children who drink before age fifteen are four times more likely to develop alcoholism than those who do not consume alcohol until the legal age of twenty-one.

In various ways then, alcoholic parents model behavior that leads children to believe that drinking often and a lot is normal. However, there are many other ways in which a person learns about alcohol.

Society

In the 1996 Roper Youth Report poll, young people who were surveyed also listed these other influential factors in shaping their drinking attitudes: best friends (28 percent), teachers (9 percent), television (7 percent), and alcohol advertisements (4 percent). These are all elements that make up the society in which an individual lives.

In the *Encyclopedic Handbook of Alcoholism,* Dwight B. Heath explains that society influences a person's drinking attitudes as surely as other values: "Ways of drinking and of thinking about drinking are learned by individuals [in any society] within the context in which they learn ways of doing other things and of thinking about them." [36]

The Muslim religion, for example, prohibits alcohol, so people born into that faith will be taught to abstain from drinking. Also, many nations have varying attitudes and customs about drinking, from the age when authorities legally allow citizens to consume alcohol to whether it is customary for people to drink alcoholic beverages with a meal. All of these differences can influence whether someone will develop a drinking problem.

However, the elements of society that can influence someone the most—besides his or her family—are friends and acquaintances. Young people especially tend to do what their friends do because they want to fit in. Paul, a Native American raised on a small Indian reservation, began his descent into alcoholism when he started drinking with friends:

> My first drunk was in the summer of my twelfth year, when I ventured to town with some friends. We purchased [alcohol] and found a place to drink it. I got drunk, blacked out, and got sick, and we went back to get some more. The accepted attitude was: "When you take a drink, you're supposed to get drunk." [37]

Paul's friends not only helped shape his viewpoint about drinking—that it was a waste of time unless one got drunk—but also helped him get alcohol illegally. This is one example of how peer pressure can lead people to drink.

In addition to genetics, family, and society, there is one more key risk factor in whether someone will have trouble with alcohol: their own psychological makeup.

Psychology

Once people have had their first experience with alcohol, they must decide if they ever want to drink again. One of the biggest factors in this decision is how alcohol affected them psychologically. James R. Milam and Katherine Ketcham explain that the main reason people like drinking is the positive effect it has on their emotions: "[They

One of the many factors leading to underage drinking is peer pressure.

want] to gain the effects of alcohol—to feel euphoric, stimulated, re-laxed, or intoxicated. Sometimes to ease frustrations, other times to put [themselves] in a good mood."[38] Bob, an alcoholic, states this concept in simpler terms: "I liked what it did to me."[39]

The emotional need that alcohol satisfies will vary from individual to individual, but most people say alcohol lessens anxiety and tension. Addiction expert Harry Milt says the danger in drinking to feel better is that people become conditioned to drink whenever they feel anxious or tense:

> The drinker has other choices for the relief of anxiety, but such relief would be in the future. The immediate reward (relief and pleasure) reinforces drinking as a conditioned response, narrowing down [the person's response to anxiety] to just this one. Once established, the drinking response is triggered by the slightest twinge of anxiety, depression, or frustration.[40]

Drinking offers only temporary relief from greater problems. This woman suffers from depression.

When people rely on alcohol to change their mood or to feel better, they will drink all the time. If they have the added weight of a family connection, friends who drink, and so forth, the end result is likely to be addiction.

Addiction Is Simple

The various factors that can increase someone's risk of becoming addicted are all in place the first time he or she takes a drink. And once some people begin drinking, there is often little they can do to stop. An ancient Japanese proverb captures the essence of this process of liquid destruction with poetic simplicity: "First man takes the drink. Then drink takes the drink. Then drink takes the man."[41]

Chapter 4

How Alcohol Ruins Lives

Nobody ever takes their first drink with the intention of one day becoming an alcoholic. Dr. Alan I. Leshner, director of the National Institute on Drug Abuse, explains that addiction is something that sneaks up on most people: "This unexpected consequence is what I have come to call the oops phenomenon. Why oops? Because the harmful outcome is in no way intentional."[42]

Unintentional though it may be, alcohol addiction does indeed cause great harm. Wendy's story is an example of how alcohol can ruin a life. Wendy had her first drink at age thirteen at a school dance on her first date. Her initial experience with alcohol was so enjoyable that she kept drinking. Within three years her life had changed—and not for the better. Wendy explains:

> At first [drinking] was on a rare basis. And then it became almost a daily thing that you start looking forward to. I mean, it just slowly takes over your life. You don't know that it's beginning to take a priority, except one day you wake up and you know you've got to have it, because you can't function [without it]. Alcohol gradually replaced everything in my life that I loved.[43]

Wendy had become an alcoholic. In the process, she was transformed from good student to dropout. She lost most of her friends and hated herself for what she was doing. When people become addicted to alcohol they not only lose control over their drinking, but they also lose control over themselves.

The long-term effects of heavy drinking are dangerous, debilitating, and deadly, and they can ruin lives in many ways. Prolonged, excessive drinking can destroy a person's health by causing a host of illnesses including cirrhosis of the liver, a disease that is often fatal. Alcohol tears apart families and weakens or destroys personal relationships, impairs job performance and can lead to dismissal from work, and creates a host of problems ranging from trouble with the law to financial ruin.

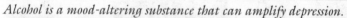

Alcohol is a mood-altering substance that can amplify depression.

A Progressive Disease

Alcoholism is a progressive disease, one that grows stronger the longer that people drink heavily. Although most of the devastating consequences of heavy drinking take time to develop—usually many years, people can start having problems right away. John grew up in a nondrinking home, but on his first night away at college he had a chance to drink for the first time. The experience was a disaster:

> I went to what they called a "kegger." Some older students had bought a keg of beer and set it up down by a river. It was the first time I ever had a beer and I drank so much I passed out. My roommates had to carry me back to our dorm. I was never so sick as I was that next day. Passing out like that scared me, sure, but a few days later I went to another one.[44]

Even though John's initial experience was frightening, he kept on drinking. Eventually, he became an alcoholic. Like many young people who drink for the first time, he did not realize how dangerous it is to consume large quantities of alcohol. This lack of knowledge can lead to disaster. During the 2000 fall college semester, at least eleven students died from alcohol-related causes at Colgate University in New York, Old Dominion University in Virginia, the University of Michigan, and Washington State University.

Once a person begins drinking, the progression into alcoholism will be different for everyone. Some people drink heavily every day, others binge several nights a week, and a smaller number go on extended drinking sprees months apart. No matter which path an alcoholic takes, there comes a time when the urge to drink becomes compulsive. Michael, who drank for more than twenty years, explains: "In the end, I'd drink by myself. I'd hide beer in the closets, under the porch of the house. It wasn't fun anymore. It went from a luxury to a must."[45]

Life Problems

Although there are many unpleasant short-term consequences—from a punishing hangover to the possibility of being arrested for drunk driving—most of the devastating outcomes of heavy drinking take time to develop. These problems become progressively more serious as alcohol steadily destroys the drinker's ability to function in every phase of his or her life, whether as a worker, family member, or friend. Many alcoholics, for example, have trouble doing their jobs and often miss days at work because they are sick or drunk. "I'd stay out late," admitted Barbara. "I found myself losing jobs."[46]

Alcoholics, through their drinking, often injure family and personal relationships by killing the love these people have for them. Their drinking hurts family members, who anguish over seeing loved ones slowly destroy themselves with alcohol. When they are confronted with their excessive drinking, many drinkers react angrily or, like Jim, start covering up their alcohol use:

> I would hide bottles all over the house and tell my wife I wasn't going to have anything to drink at night except two beers. Then when she was on the phone or taking a bath, I'd run get a bottle and take a big drink. She smelled alcohol on my breath, but she figured it was only the beer. I lied like that for years.[47]

Alcoholics, however, are almost always trapped by their lies. When Jim's wife found bottles he had stashed in various places, they fought. Not only injured by his drinking but also by his lies, she lost faith in Jim because she never knew when he was telling the truth. Many alcoholics wind up divorced because their spouses cannot bear living with them. If alcoholics remain married, their relationships are often troubled, with the anger sometimes spilling over into domestic violence. Studies have shown that 67 percent of people who attacked their spouse or other intimate partner had been drinking.

Alcohol can also destroy friendships. Friends can turn away from an alcoholic because they do not like drinking themselves or because they hate the way that person is acting. For example, many alcoholics have financial problems. They often borrow money from family or friends but never repay it. Jerry remembers how he was always asking for loans during his drinking days:

> I always needed money, even though I spent most of it on booze. I borrowed from friends, other guys at the bar, people at work, anyone who would give me a few bucks. I never had any when it came time to pay them back. I made a lot of people mad at me, one guy even threatened to beat me up. It wasn't a good way to live, but I didn't care as long as I had money to drink.[48]

Alcoholics have trouble with relationships because people who drink heavily are very volatile, with anger and resentment the two most common emotions fueling their actions. Alcoholics often blow up over small events, becoming enraged over minor incidents that most people would accept, such as a flat tire. The resulting out-of-control behavior—shouting, abusive language, displays of temper such as throwing things—can alienate everyone around them.

Poor Decisions

The difficulty alcoholics have in controlling their emotions often leads them to make one poor choice after another. This may include

Alcohol-induced arguments can create larger problems in a relationship.

Drunk driving is a leading cause of vehicular accidents.

driving while drunk—which not only endangers the alcoholic but many other people as well. In 1998 alone, alcohol-related accidents killed 15,935 Americans and injured another 305,000. Drinking is also a factor in one-third of all drownings and boating and aviation deaths as well as many other types of accidental fatalities. Harry Milt, in *Alcoholism, Its Causes and Cure: A New Handbook,* explains that alcohol greatly relaxes a person's normal sense of inhibition and restraint: "Cheating and stealing are no longer out of the question. . . . In general, the disinhibiting effect of alcohol enables the drinker to do things he wanted to do while sober but could not do because of conscience, shame, guilt, fear, prudence, or common sense."[49]

This lack of inhibition leads people to do stupid things. Author Susan Brink lists some of the humiliating, disturbing actions that people she interviewed for a magazine article on alcoholism admitted they did:

> Inga fell down a flight of stairs with her infant in her arms. Mark had five wives, and five divorces. Betty polished off a pint of vodka, then carpooled fourth graders from soccer practice. Jeffrey committed strong-armed robbery. April, once shy, took off her clothes and danced for money. Martha threat-

ened her husband with a carving knife. Paula slipped into the kitchen during dinner parties to swill down the last drops of wine left in dirty goblets. All are recovering alcoholics and they are ashamed of these recollections.[50]

When people are drunk, they may also decide to do dangerous things. Padric, a gay teenage alcoholic, admits that, "I drank to get up the courage to do dangerous things."[51] He remembers that he often got into troubling situations when looking for partners in bars. Wendy, the young girl who dropped out of school when drinking began to consume her life, had several close calls with death. While drunk, she once almost died after she fell four stories from the window ledge of a Brooklyn brownstone while trying to attract her boyfriend's attention. She also cut her face with a razor blade while

---

"Getting Stupid" on Alcohol

Some teenagers jokingly refer to drinking a lot as "getting stupid." Young people, however, have no idea how accurate that slang term is. In an article in *Discover* magazine, Bernice Wuethrich explains that young people who drink may damage their brains, which are still growing and developing and are thus more sensitive to alcohol than those of adults. Therefore, when teenagers drink, the consequence may be a loss of as much as 10 percent of their mental ability.

Scientists have long known that excessive alcohol consumption among adults over long periods of time can create brain damage, ranging from a mild loss of motor skills to psychosis and even the inability to form memories. But less has been known about the impact alcohol has on younger brains. Until recently, scientists assumed that a youthful brain is more resilient than an adult brain and could escape many of the worst ills of alcohol. But some researchers are now beginning to question this assumption. Preliminary results from several studies indicate that the younger the brain is, the more it may be at risk. "The adolescent brain is a developing nervous system, and the things you do to it can change it," says Scott Swartzwelder, a neuropsychologist at Duke University. Teen drinkers appear to be most susceptible to damage in the hippocampus, a structure buried deep in the brain that is responsible for many types of learning and memory, and the prefrontal cortex, located behind the forehead, which is the brain's chief decision maker and voice of reason. Both areas, especially the prefrontal cortex, undergo dramatic change in the second decade of life. When Swartzwelder published his first paper [in 1995] suggesting that alcohol disrupts the hippocampus more severely in adolescents, "people didn't believe it," he says. Since then, his research has shown that the adolescent brain is more easily damaged in the structures that regulate the acquisition and storage of memories.

drunk. "It's insanity that happens when you're in the throes of this disease," Wendy admitted. "I didn't want to cut myself up; I didn't want to jump out windows."[52]

The inability to think clearly and make proper decisions can also lead people to do things they know are wrong, not just morally but legally. This can be seen in the well-established link between alcohol and crime.

Alcohol and Crime

Research shows that alcohol use is involved in one-half of all crimes committed in America. A study by the National Institute on Drug Abuse and the National Institute on Alcohol Abuse and Alcoholism (NIAAA) estimated that in 1992 the cost to U.S. society of crimes attributed to alcohol, ranging from robbery to homicide, was $19.7 billion. That included medical bills and lost work days for victims,

A policeman arrests a drunken fan after a Super Bowl game.

damage to property, and the cost to incarcerate offenders. Almost one-quarter of the 11.1 million victims of violent crime each year report that the offender had been drinking, and studies show that the amount of alcohol consumed is related to the severity of the subsequent violence.

Research figures in the *Tenth Special Report to the U.S. Congress on Alcohol and Health* indicate that people who were intoxicated committed 15 percent of the robberies, 26 percent of the aggravated and simple assaults, 37 percent of the rapes and sexual assaults, and 32 percent of the homicides in cases studied. Figures showed that more people committed crimes while under the influence of alcohol than while using any other drug: "Thus, despite the popular conception that violent crime is strongly linked to drug use, there is actually a much greater probability that any given violent incident will be related to alcohol use than to [other] drugs."[53]

Alcohol Kills

The physical effects of chronic alcohol abuse are wide-ranging and complex because alcohol reaches every cell and organ of the body. Alcohol damages the liver, the central nervous system, the gastrointestinal tract, and the heart. People who drink heavily for a long period generally decrease their life expectancy by ten to fifteen years. The NIAAA estimates that more than ninety thousand Americans die each year from alcohol-related diseases. This figure is about 5 percent of all deaths in the United States, ranking alcohol use as the fourth major cause of death in America.

Heavy drinking causes so many physical problems that about 40 percent of all hospital admissions are alcohol-related, and alcoholics use health services at twice the rate of the general population. The most common and serious health problems occur in the liver, which performs many essential functions and is vital to life. It breaks down proteins, carbohydrates, and fats from food so the body can use them, stores vitamins and other substances the body needs, removes waste and toxic matter from the blood, and regulates blood volume.

One of the substances the liver breaks down so the body can use it is alcohol, but chemical by-products from this process can damage the organ. Exposure to these chemical by-products can inflame the

Large quantities of alcohol can destroy a liver. Compare the normal liver (left) to the liver in the middle, fatty from alcohol comsumption, and to the liver on the right, cirrhotic from alcohol abuse.

liver, make it larger, and reduce its ability to function, which will make the drinker ill. The most severe form of liver damage is called cirrhosis, which means the liver has become scarred because individual cells are being killed. Each year more than twenty-five thousand Americans die from alcohol-induced liver problems.

Because diseased livers grow larger and become tender, alcoholics often know there is damage before they ever see a doctor. The sensations of discomfort they feel from their malfunctioning livers are often the first warning signs they have that their drinking is beginning to harm them. Joe, who drank heavily for nearly two decades, explains what it felt like:

> I knew there was something wrong. My side was always sore and at night I couldn't sleep on it [his side] because it hurt. And not long after I would start drinking, I could feel it [his liver] beating, throbbing. I guess it was processing the alcohol. It felt funny. It scared me, too, but by that time I didn't know how to do anything else but keep on drinking.[54]

Unlike some alcoholics who destroy their livers and die unless they have a transplant, Joe did not have any permanent damage, probably because the liver has a tremendous capacity to regenerate itself. But there is another major organ that is heavily affected by alcohol that cannot heal itself—the brain.

Alcohol and the Brain

Research has proven that continued exposure to large amounts of alcohol causes significant changes in the brain's physical structure and impairs how it functions. These changes include modifications in the shape of brain cells and a noticeable shrinking of the brain itself; autopsies of alcoholics have consistently shown their brains to be smaller and lighter than those of other people of the same age and gender.

A reduction in brain size is just one of many changes caused by heavy drinking, none of them healthy. Studies indicate that 50 to 75 percent of heavy drinkers show some kind of impairment in the way they think and reason, even after they detoxify and abstain from alcohol. And according to the NIAAA, alcoholic dementia is the second-leading cause of adult dementia in the United States, accounting for 10 percent of such cases and second only to Alzheimer's disease.

Dementia is a condition in which the brain's ability to function has been reduced. This can adversely affect a person's ability to remember things, to understand abstract concepts, to speak clearly, and to perform fine physical movements, impairments that make it harder for people to function normally. Approximately 9 percent of alcoholics have brain damage severe enough to be diagnosed by a doctor, and 50 to 75 percent of alcoholics have some degree of brain damage.

One of the most severe forms of brain damage from excessive alcohol use is known as alcoholic Korsakoff's syndrome. It is characterized, in part, by an inability to remember recent events or to learn new information. In 1976 an interview with Mr. F., a fifty-eight-year-old patient at a Veterans Administration Hospital in Boston who had been diagnosed with Korsakoff's syndrome, showed how decades of heavy drinking had destroyed this World War II soldier's memory. Although Gerald Ford was president, the patient did not know it:

DOCTOR: Do you know who the president of the United States is?

MR. F.: Let's see, uh. . . .

DOCTOR: The president of the United States.

MR. F.: [Harry] Truman?

DOCTOR: Truman. Well, Truman goes back quite a while ago. There must be someone else.

MR. F.: [Dwight] Eisenhower?

DOCTOR: Uh-uh. Who else? Who is president right now?

MR. F.: Beats me. [55]

Heavy alcohol consumption can also contribute to or cause many other health problems, including heart damage, high blood pressure, and an increased risk for coronary artery disease and stroke. Long-term excessive drinking has also been linked to the risk of developing certain forms of cancer, especially cancer of the esophagus, mouth, throat, and voice box.

Drinkers also risk one other serious health problem. The risk, however, is not to the drinker but to an unborn child.

Fetal Alcohol Syndrome

Fetal alcohol syndrome (FAS) is the name for a group of physical and mental birth defects that are the direct result of a woman's drinking alcohol during pregnancy. An FAS child can be mentally retarded or have reduced mental abilities, growth deficiencies, central nervous system dysfunction, abnormally shaped heads and faces, and behavioral problems. Fetal alcohol effect (FAE) is a less severe set of the same symptoms. More than five thousand children are born in the United States each year with FAS, the most common nonhereditary form of mental retardation.

First identified in France in 1968, it was not until several years later that U.S. researchers began to study FAS. Up until then, it

This young boy's face shows signs of fetal alcohol syndrome.

was not known that pregnant women could injure a fetus by drinking, and pregnant women were often advised to have a glass of wine or a drink to relax them or help them sleep. But researchers now believe that even moderate drinking can create permanent disabilities, and doctors advise pregnant women to abstain from alcohol.

Fetal Alcohol Syndrome

The National Organization on Fetal Alcohol Syndrome (NOFAS) works to educate the public about this alcohol-related birth defect. The following is information on the syndrome from the group's website.

Fetal Alcohol Syndrome is a series of mental and physical birth defects that can include mental retardation, growth deficiencies, central nervous system dysfunction, craniofacial abnormalities and behavioral maladjustments. Fetal Alcohol Effect is a less severe set of the same symptoms. If you drink wine, beer, or liquor when you are pregnant, your baby could develop FAS. A baby with FAS [will have] disabilities that will last a lifetime. No amount of alcohol has been proven safe to consume during pregnancy. FAS and FAE (Fetal Alcohol Effects) are 100% preventable when a pregnant woman abstains from alcohol. At least 5,000 infants are born each year with FAS, or approximately one out of every 750 live births. Thirty to forty percent of babies whose mothers drink heavily throughout pregnancy have the Syndrome. FAS/FAE is a problem found in all races and socio-economic groups. FAS and FAE are widely under diagnosed. Some experts believe between one-third and two-thirds of all children in special education have been affected by alcohol in some way. The institutional and medical costs for one child with FAS are $1.4 million over a lifetime. Is there a cure for FAS? There is no cure for Fetal Alcohol Syndrome. Once the damage is done, it cannot be undone. However, FAS is the only cause of birth defects that can be completely prevented. How can FAS be prevented? The easiest way for a woman to prevent FAS is to not drink during pregnancy.

The birth defects FAS creates can ruin the lives of its victims and their parents. Nasdijj was born with fetal alcohol syndrome. He states, "My mother was a Navajo drunk. I cannot recall her ever being sober."[56] When Nasdijj married, he and his wife adopted an infant boy who, unknown to them, suffered from FAS. The boy, named Tommy Nothing Fancy, died at age six from FAS complications. Nasdijj still struggles with the birth defect:

I have FAS. Not as badly as Tommy Nothing Fancy had it. My version of the disease manifests itself in some rather severe learning disabilities. All my craziness, my inability to deal with authority, my perceptual malfunctions, my upside-down imagery (I can read entire books upside down), my rage, comes from FAS. I have never held a real job for more than a year in my life. Reading and writing are complete tortures for me, so I could understand how it was torture for my son.[57]

Dangerous Alcohol

Alcohol can ruin innocent lives as well as those of alcoholics who, drink by drink, take part in their own destruction. Enoch Gordis, director of the NIAAA, says simply that "alcohol is the most widespread and damaging substance we have in society."[58]

Chapter 5

Alcohol: Treating the Disease

For much of the first half of the twentieth century, people who wanted to quit drinking had a difficult time finding help. Pulitzer Prize–winning journalist and novelist Nan Robertson, who fought and won her own battle with alcoholism, describes the few dismal options available to alcoholics of that period to aid them in dealing with their problem:

> There were only two ways for a drunk to go if the family wouldn't take care of him or he couldn't afford a "drink cure" in a fancy sanitarium—to the drunk tank in jail or to the insane asylum. In those days alcoholics who wound up in [mental institutions] were locked in wards with criminal psychopaths and those afflicted with senile dementia. Nobody knew what else to do with them. [59]

Until the American Medical Association officially recognized alcoholism as a disease during the 1960s, most people believed that drunkards (the term once used to refer to alcoholics) drank because they were morally degenerate and that it was a waste of time to try to help them. This belief is embodied in the comments of J. E. Todd, a Connecticut doctor who, on June 21, 1882, cruelly proclaimed, "Every human soul is worth saving; but what I mean is, that if a choice is to be made, drunkards are about the last class to be taken hold of." [60]

Attitudes changed dramatically once the medical establishment and society in general began to believe that people drank uncontrollably because they were suffering from an illness and not because they had character flaws that made them morally inferior. In *Contested Meanings: The Construction of Alcohol Problems*, Joseph R. Gusfield explains this transformation:

> For the nineteenth century and the first third of the twentieth, the habitual drunkard was someone to be condemned as a sinner and pitied for his moral limitations. He bore the stigma of the sinner. With the disease theory of alcoholism, he was a victim of illness . . . he was an object of help, not condemnation.[61]

Passersby glare at a fall-down drunk in 1943.

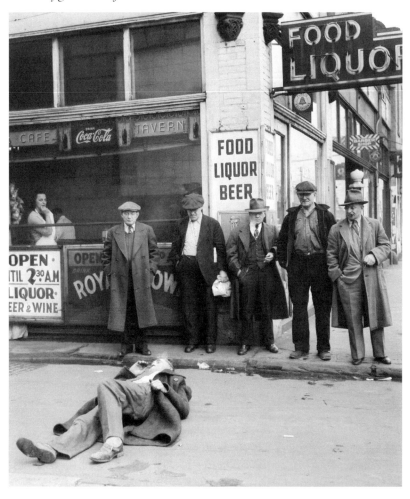

Do You Have A Drinking Problem?

Many tests can help people determine if they have a drinking problem. This test, which uses a simple question-and-answer format, can be found in a booklet entitled "Alcoholism" from the National Institute on Alcohol Abuse and Alcoholism.

How can you tell whether you, or someone close to you, may have a drinking problem? Answering the following four questions can help you find out. (To help remember these questions, note that the first letter of a key word in each of the four questions spells "CAGE.")

Have you ever felt you should Cut down on your drinking?

Have people Annoyed you by criticizing your drinking?

Have you ever felt bad or Guilty about your drinking?

Have you ever had a drink first thing in the morning to steady your nerves or to get rid of a hangover (Eyeopener)?

One "yes" response suggests a possible alcohol problem. If you responded "yes" to more than one question, it is highly likely that a problem exists. In either case, it is important that you see your doctor or other health care provider right away to discuss your responses to these questions. He or she can help you determine whether you have a drinking problem and, if so, recommend the best course of action for you. Even if you answered "no" to all of the above questions, if you are encountering drinking-related problems with your job, relationships, health, or with the law, you should still seek professional help. The effects of alcohol abuse can be extremely serious—even fatal—both to you and to others.

It is now generally accepted that alcoholism is an illness, one that can be treated like any other disease, and alcoholics today who want to quit have a wide variety of treatment options from which to choose. However, no treatment will ever work until the alcoholic acknowledges the depth of his or her drinking problems. For most alcoholics, this step does not come easily.

Denial

Many alcoholics—even those who have been fired from jobs, have been jailed for drunk driving, and have lost the love of their family and friends because of their drinking—cannot admit the damage done by their alcohol use. This attitude is commonly known as *denial*. Barbara McCrady, a professor of psychology and the clinical director of the Center for Alcohol Studies at Rutgers University in New Brunswick, New Jersey, explains that denial is the biggest obstacle to recovery facing an alcoholic: "If a person doesn't recognize that his or her behavior is creating problems, then he or she wouldn't see the need to change or seek assistance."[62]

Alcoholics use denial as a psychological defense mechanism to justify their continued drinking and to wipe away the painful reality of their drinking. This is how denial worked in the mind of Chris, who, despite her heavy drinking, believed her life was perfectly normal:

> I went to Girl Scout meetings with a load on; held children's parties while imbibing; even taught my daughter how to drive after I had belted down a few. My marriage was horrendous, and I saw no way out. And yet I still believed I was the All-American Housewife.[63]

Sometimes the only way to get alcoholics to realize they have a problem is to directly confront them with their drinking. This can be a difficult, emotionally wrenching task for the people who are involved in trying to save the alcoholic.

Intervention

Interventions are important because they can help alcoholics overcome their denial about the problems caused by their drinking. In an intervention, family members, friends, coworkers, and other key people in the drinker's life band together to talk to the individual about how his or her drinking is affecting them.

Whether this is done in a doctor's office, a hospital, or at the person's home, it can be an extremely painful experience for everyone involved. The alcoholic may break down in tears when loved ones explain how the drinker's behavior has hurt them, and they may also be crying because of the outpouring of pent-up emotions. Interventions can also be angry affairs; the alcoholic may continue denying the problem, and other people may be overcome by resentment or bitterness in discussing all of the things the drinker has done to ruin their lives.

Former first lady Betty Ford, who has spoken publicly about her drinking, admits she was upset at first when confronted by members of her family and others. Recalls Ford, "All of them hurt me [with their stories about Ford's drinking]. I collapsed into tears. But I still had enough sense to realize they hadn't come around just to make me cry; they were there because they loved me and wanted to help me."[64] The intervention made Ford realize how severe her drinking had become and she sought treatment and was able to quit.

The most important step drinkers take toward recovery is to finally admit to themselves, as Ford did, that they have to quit. Although alcoholics will need a great deal of help to do this, fortunately today they have a wide variety of care options from which to choose.

Betty Ford leaves a hospital in 1978 after being treated for alcoholism and drug addiction.

Intervention

Because so many alcoholics refuse to admit they have a problem, an intervention is often useful in making them realize the tragic consequences of their drinking. In *Alcohol Problems and Alcoholism: A Comprehensive Survey*, James E. Royce discusses this form of encounter.

> Very often the most effective way to motivate a person to go into treatment is by a group confrontation. This must be carefully planned, under the guidance of a trained alcoholism worker. It is useful to have each family member write out and read a list of times and events [involving the person's drinking], which makes the encounter less emotional and more factual. Since they know about it anyhow, small children can have a powerful role to play, as when daddy's girl says, "Why do you drink that stuff when it makes you talk so funny or hurt mommy?" Significant others besides family members may be able to make a useful contribution. The alcoholic will try to play the confronters off against one another. Each must agree to maintain a united front; no one party can feel sorry for the alcoholic and spoil the unanimity. The alcoholic will cry, accuse them of picking on him or her, of being unfair, of exaggerating, etc. But they must promise not to settle for anything less than agreement to enter treatment. It must be explained.

Detox

The first step for many alcoholics is a detoxification center—a medical facility where medical personnel help them sober up and treat them for the physical symptoms brought on by alcohol withdrawal. It can take anywhere from three to six days for heavy drinkers to purge all of the alcohol from their bodies. During this period, which is known as withdrawal, alcoholics can suffer severe, even life-threatening physical and psychological reactions.

The symptoms of withdrawal include trouble sleeping, disorientation, hallucinations, convulsions, and seizures. The most extreme form of withdrawal is known as delirium tremens, DTs, a condition that is accompanied by acute anxiety and fear, agitation, fast pulse, fever, extreme perspiration, and hallucinations. Detoxification centers are staffed by doctors and other personnel who monitor and help alcoholics with their withdrawal symptoms. In severe cases, doctors can administer medication to lessen the symptoms.

Once detoxification is complete, alcoholics can seek help in many different settings. Hospitals, private clinics, residential facilities, self-help

Alcoholics meet for support in a hospital where they are being detoxified.

groups, and private medical practitioners all offer programs aimed at helping alcoholics stop drinking. In the United States, it is estimated that each day more than seven hundred thousand people receive medical help for alcohol addiction. By far the largest number of alcoholics seek treatment through outpatient programs. In outpatient programs, alcoholics visit a care center for only part of the day to receive counseling and help in quitting.

Treatment programs almost always include alcohol education classes and some form of group or individual therapy. In individual sessions, only the patient and therapist are present. In group therapy sessions, patients share their experiences, feelings, and concerns with other alcoholics. In both cases, the discussion is usually guided by a trained therapist, sometimes a psychologist, psychiatrist, or counselor.

One of the most important aspects of group therapy is that the alcoholic realizes that he or she is not alone in fighting the disease, that many other people have been struggling for years with the same problem. Jane, a recovering alcoholic, explains how such sessions helped her:

> Listening to other people talk about what happened to them, I realized I wasn't the only one who had this problem. There were other people who drank too much and wanted to quit but couldn't. That made me feel better. The most amazing thing was that even though everyone was different, they all had pretty much the same things happen to them, and I could understand just how they felt.[65]

Outpatient programs offer services of varying intensity and duration, some for only for a few hours several days a week. The patient visits the care center for these sessions but does not stay there overnight. All programs try to help alcoholics understand how alcohol addiction works and how to deal with it in their daily lives. Treatment is based on the experiences of recovering alcoholics and the professional staff treating them as well as research on human behavior.

Some treatment centers also prescribe drugs to help people stay sober. One commonly used drug is Antabuse, which reacts with alcohol to make people sick if they drink. Recent research has led to the development of other drugs that can help ease the drinker's craving for alcohol. One such promising drug is Naltrexone, which helps quell both the physical and psychological components of this terrible compulsion.

Although treatment programs vary in the forms of care they give recovering alcoholics, one aspect of treatment is a given for almost everyone: an introduction to the concepts of the self-help group known as Alcoholics Anonymous (AA). This group's principles are universally accepted and taught in alcohol treatment programs, almost all of which recommend that their patients attend AA meetings to stay sober.

Alcoholics Anonymous

AA is based on the simple premise that to stay sober, alcoholics must help other alcoholics. AA was founded in 1935 by two alcoholics who had struggled with their drinking for decades: Bill Wilson, a failed New York businessman, and Robert Smith, an Akron, Ohio, doctor. Wilson, who had been confined to mental institutions and hospitals several times because of his drinking, created AA's twelve steps, which form the basis of the AA recovery program. The twelve steps outline the actions people need to take to quit drinking and learn to live a sober lifestyle.

The first and most important step is for people to admit they are powerless over alcohol and that drinking has created so many severe

A woman talks with a counselor at an alcoholism treatment center. The books in the foreground are publications of Alcoholics Anonymous.

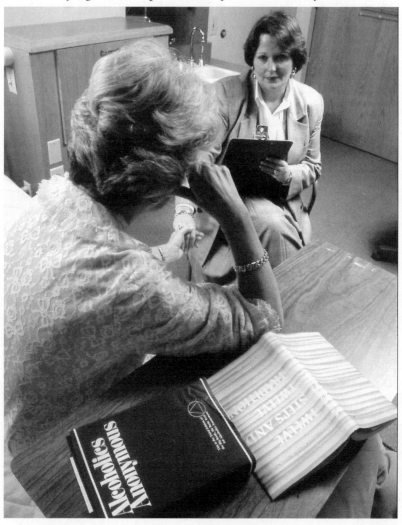

Bill W. and Dr. Bob

The cover of the June 14, 1999, issue of *Time* is a collage of famous people the magazine considers "Heroes and Icons," including boxer Muhammad Ali, slain President John F. Kennedy, and Mother Teresa. One space, however, was left blank in honor of Bill Wilson, the cofounder of Alcoholics Anonymous. Although famed philosopher Aldous Huxley once called Wilson "the greatest social architect of [the twentieth] century," Wilson always shunned personal publicity out of a fear that it might endanger the organization he helped create. Wilson asked the media to refer to him as "Bill W.," and Robert Smith became "Dr. Bob." A story in the magazine by novelist Susan Cheever, herself a recovering alcoholic, explains how AA got its start after the two men met.

> Five months [after quitting drinking], Wilson went to Akron, Ohio, on business. The deal fell through, and he wanted a drink. He stood in the lobby of the Mayflower Hotel, entranced by the sounds of the bar across the hall. Suddenly he became convinced that by helping another alcoholic, he could save himself. Through a series of desperate phone calls, he found Dr. Robert Smith, a skeptical drunk whose family persuaded him to give Wilson 15 minutes. Their meeting lasted four hours. A month later, Dr. Bob had his last drink, and that date, June 10, 1935, is the official birth date of A.A., which is based on the idea that only an alcoholic can help another alcoholic. "Because of our kinship in suffering," Bill wrote, "our channels of contact have always been charged with the language of the heart."

problems in their lives that they must quit. The other steps include a personal inventory of how they harmed themselves and other people, with an emphasis on how anger, fear, resentment, and selfishness influenced their actions. The alcoholics also list everyone hurt by their drinking and try to make amends. The alcoholic must also work to conquer characteristics that contribute to his or her drinking. The steps are done progressively, but a member of AA is never completely done with any of them. Recovering alcoholics continue trying to understand the steps more deeply and working them more perfectly for the rest of their lives so they can remain sober.

The heart of the AA program is a belief that alcoholics need the help of a "higher power" to quit drinking and transform their lives for the better in many other ways. AA, however, is not a religious program. It is not allied with any specific religious group, and its members include Catholics, Protestants, Jews, and members of other major religions. The pamphlet *Forty-four Questions* explains that AA only asks that its members believe in a higher power as they understand it:

> Most members, before turning to A.A., had already admitted that they could not control their drinking. Alcohol had become a power greater than themselves, and it had been accepted on those terms. A.A. suggests that to achieve and maintain sobriety, alcoholics need to accept and depend upon another Power recognized as greater than themselves. [66]

AA members are urged to develop a one-on-one dialogue with the higher power of their choosing. To make themselves strong enough to stay sober and lead better lives, AA members maintain this vital link to their higher power by daily prayer, inspirational readings, and meditation.

How AA Works

Alcoholics Anonymous began after Wilson and Smith met in Akron and began talking to each other about how alcohol had ruined their lives. Since that time, Alcoholics Anonymous has grown into a worldwide organization that operates in 150 countries and has over 2 million members. Its strength still comes from the simple principle that alcoholics must help other alcoholics in order to stay sober. The best description of this is from the preamble that is usually read before each AA meeting:

> Alcoholics Anonymous is a fellowship of men and women who share their experience, strength and hope with each other that they may solve their common problem and help others to recover from alcoholism. The only requirement for membership is a desire to stop drinking. Our primary purpose is to stay sober and help other alcoholics to achieve sobriety. [67]

Anyone who believes they have a drinking problem can attend meetings, which usually last one hour and generally include readings from *Alcoholics Anonymous* or other literature. There are no dues or fees for membership in AA, although people usually make a small voluntary contribution when they attend meetings to cover incidental costs such as renting a room and serving coffee.

The most important part of the meeting, which is similar to group therapy, is when members have a chance to explain how they are staying sober, comment on one of the steps, or simply talk about something that is bothering them. This sharing, as it is called, helps others realize they are not alone in battling alcohol, provides them with the hope that they can stay sober, and shows them ways that other people have managed their sobriety.

Alcoholics Anonymous has proven to be the most effective long-term form of treatment for alcoholism. In fact, AA has been so successful in helping alcoholics that its twelve steps have been adopted

An Alcoholics Anonymous (AA) meeting. In AA, alcoholics gather to share their stories and help each other stay sober.

by groups fighting many other addictions, from narcotics abuse to overeating. The *Columbia University College of Physicians and Surgeons Complete Home Medical Guide* claims,

> Alcoholics Anonymous and its subgroups—Al-Anon for family members of alcoholics and Alateen for teenage children of alcoholics—are self-help organizations that provide experienced advice and support for alcoholics and their families. Most experts recognize A.A. as the core of any alcoholic therapy.[68]

Relapse

Neither AA nor any other program can help everyone. And for many alcoholics, the battle to quit can be a long one, with both victories and defeats. When an alcoholic resumes drinking it is called relapse. And relapse is common, even for people who have been hospitalized several times in their fight to stop. Author Arnold M. Ludwig says staying sober is difficult because the craving for alcohol results in people making excuses that justify drinking:

> The alcoholic's worst enemy is not the bottle but his own mind, within which is the ever-present Trojan horse of desire, waiting to smuggle in the enemy when the defenses have been lulled into complacency. What must be recognized is that in this case the brain is much less an organ of rationality than of rationalization. His mind tries to legitimize his intentions and behaviors so that he need not feel guilty. So that he can convince himself that he is making the right choice.[69]

In addition to the internal struggles and cravings that often rage in the minds of alcoholics, many social pressures can entice people to drink again. Sometimes promptings from friends or family members who have their own problems with alcohol are all that is needed to start someone drinking again. Nicholas A. Pace of New York, an assistant professor at the New York University School of Medicine, says that to stay sober, people need to make drastic changes in their lives, including changing with whom they socialize:

> Patients need to examine their drinking or drugging lives carefully to decide what situations may have stimulated them to use. Maybe they'll find that every time they went to visit their mother they got into an argument and started to drink. If that's the case, it's probably not such a good idea for them to visit their mother in early sobriety or until they've worked with a therapist through the issues that cause these arguments. Like they say in A.A., stay away from or avoid the people, places and things that are going to remind you of drinking.[70]

Sobriety Success

Alcoholism treatment is helping more alcoholics today than ever before to quit drinking. The *Tenth Special Report to the U.S. Congress on Alcohol and Health,* issued in 2000 by the National Institutes of Health and the NIAAA, states, "Treatment outcome studies have repeatedly found large and sustained reductions in drinking among persons seeking help for alcoholism."[71]

Treatment does not help everyone, however. It is generally believed that out of one hundred people in addiction treatment, about a third will quit, another third will reduce their drug use, and the remainder will continue using drugs or drinking. Alcoholics Anonymous is the most successful long-term recovery program. But even AA estimates that only 10 percent of alcoholics ever attend a meeting and only about 10 percent of those remain sober more than three months before relapsing. These figures suggest that alcoholics can stop drinking, but not without a great deal of effort and determination.

Chapter 6

A History of Regulation

Unlike other addictive drugs such as marijuana, cocaine, and heroin, alcohol is legal to use and can be easily purchased by adults in the United States almost anywhere and at any time. People routinely buy a six-pack of beer along with a gallon of milk at their corner grocery store or even when they stop at a gas station. Dr. Gail Gleason Milgram calls alcohol "the drug of choice for most Americans."[72]

Yet America is also the nation that early in the twentieth century believed alcohol was such a menace to the well-being of its citizens that it banned the manufacture and sale of this drug during what was known as Prohibition. This unique effort in social engineering began in 1919, but Prohibition had no sooner gone into effect than tens of millions of Americans began rebelling against it. Their decision to keep drinking beer, wine, and liquor even though it was illegal doomed America's attempt to eradicate alcohol, and Prohibition ended in 1933.

Although Prohibition has been dead for decades, remnants remain of the national fear that once existed regarding the harm that unlimited access to alcohol can cause people. The spirit of Prohibition still lives today in laws that restrict the sale of beer, wine, and liquor in a few states and counties scattered around the nation.

The fact that Americans are still divided over alcohol use in the twenty-first century is not surprising. In one form or another, the debate over regulating alcohol has raged in America for over two centuries. In *Understanding America's Drinking Problem: How to Combat the Hazards of Alcohol,* author Don Cahalan explains: "Ever since the Pilgrims landed at Plymouth Rock, our politicians and the rest of us have see-sawed up and down on whether and how to control alcohol problems."[73]

This float in an anti-Prohibition parade uses a quotation from the Bible to support the right to drink alcoholic beverages.

The Temperance Movement

The first colonists believed alcohol was a necessary part of life. But by the time Americans were winning their freedom from Great Britain in the Revolutionary War, many people had begun to realize that alcohol was causing severe problems. The reason was a change in drinking patterns during the eighteenth century as Americans began to drink more, especially distilled spirits such as brandy.

In some ways, this new style of drinking mirrored the earlier gin fever that had swept through Great Britain. By the 1830s the annual per capita consumption for people aged fifteen or older was 7 gallons of pure alcohol (100 percent alcohol), a quantity more than twice the current rate of 2.8 gallons, resulting from drinking an average of 9.5 gallons of spirits, 1 to 2 gallons of wine, and 27 gallons of beer. The

Members of the Women's Christian Temperance Union march on Washington, D.C., in 1909 to present a petition supporting Prohibition.

higher drinking levels led to increased public drunkenness, incidents of violence, and other social problems.

The American Society for the Promotion of Temperance, later known as the American Temperance Society (ATS), was founded in Boston in 1826 to combat the new levels of abuse of alcohol, and by 1833 six thousand local temperance societies with more than 1 million members had been formed. Most Temperance groups at first only sought to moderate and not ban drinking, but by 1836 members of ATS, which was led by Protestant clergymen, were advocating total abstinence and became known as teetotalers. The word teetotal originated in England when a man who stuttered badly backed the idea of abstinence at a temperance meeting: "We can't keep 'em sober unless we have the pledge [to quit drinking] total. Yes, Mr. Chairman, tee-tee-total."[74]

The concept that alcohol could be a harmful substance was strange to Americans in the first few decades of the nineteenth century because so many of them still believed that people needed to drink alcohol to remain healthy. The U.S. Army served daily rations of alcohol to its soldiers, and many other employers provided the same on-the-job benefit for their workers. But after the temperance movement began to grow in power, it began changing daily life in America, and by the 1830s these daily rations of alcohol were coming to an end. One New York farmer who quit giving his hired hands whiskey claimed they now "labored like sober, rational men, and not like intoxicated mutineers."[75]

One way the temperance movement tried to persuade drinkers to give up alcohol was to have them pledge to quit; as a result, millions of people "took the pledge," although many would fail to keep the promise and would later return to drinking. One of the most effective early temperance leaders was the Reverend Lyman Beecher, who advocated total abstinence with dramatic, highly effective statements such as this one: "Much is said about the prudent use of spirits, but we might as well speak of poison taken prudently every day."[76] Temperance groups also began to lobby for legislation to prohibit alcohol. The first such law was passed in New York State in 1845, but it was repealed two years later when citizens who wanted to drink complained about the legislation.

The temperance movement was strengthened during the middle of the nineteenth century when women began to assume leadership roles in fighting alcohol, making this the first time that American women became actively involved in social issues. In 1854 Susan B. Anthony, who is more famous for helping women win the right to vote, established the Woman's State Temperance Society of New York, the first such group formed by women and run by women. Another famous temperance leader was Carry Nation, whose axe-wielding protests in taverns helped popularize the issue. The most influential single group during this period, however, was the Women's Christian Temperance Union (WCTU). The WCTU, which was founded in 1841, once had over two hundred thousand dues-paying members and is still active today.

Because women could not vote during the nineteenth century, they could not directly influence elected officials to regulate alcohol consumption. Instead, they generated public outrage by staging protests aimed at saloons, which were considered as bad a problem as alcohol because they had become centers of gambling, prostitution, and other criminal activities.

These public protests peaked during the Woman's Crusade of 1873–1874 with a series of direct actions against saloons across the nation. Women sang religious hymns and held prayer vigils outside saloons (protests that helped keep patrons away), began petition drives to close saloons, and tried to win the support of local officials to regulate such establishments.

Prohibition

These crusaders managed to shut down some saloons, but not enough to ease the problem. The movement then began to fight to shut off the source of alcohol itself.

The first state prohibition law was passed in Maine in 1846, but few states did anything for decades to ease the flow of alcohol. But when the Anti-Saloon League was founded in 1893, it led a new wave of state prohibition drives that culminated in passage of the eighteenth Amendment to the Constitution, which banned the manufacture and sale of liquor in the United States for more than a decade.

The Woman's Crusade in Xenia, Ohio

During the winter of 1873–1874, the Woman's Crusade against alcohol spread across much of the northern United States as thousands of women participated in demonstrations and prayer vigils to close down saloons. The following account of one such crusade, which conveys the sense of triumph felt by those who participated, is reported by a witness in Xenia, Ohio. It is from the Ohio State University history department's Internet site on Prohibition.

> Going out I saw crowds of people thronging towards Whitman street, and heard on every hand in joyful accents, "The Shades of Death [a saloon] has surrendered!: The good news proved true, and I found Whitman street thronged with people. A little before 3 o'clock, as it appeared from the general account, Mr. Steve Phillips, of the "Shades of Death," invited the ladies to enter, and announced that he gave up everything to them, and would never sell anything intoxicating in Xenia again. Then the ladies, joined by the spectators, sang "Praise God from whom all blessings flow," while the liquors were rolled into the street. A half-barrel of blackberry brandy, the same of high-wines, a few kegs of beer, and some bottles of ale and whisky were soon emptied into the street, amid the shouts of the enthusiastic multitude. Of the women around, some were crying, some were laughing, a few alternately singing and returning thanks. One elderly lady in the edge of the crowd was almost in hysterics, but still shouting in a hoarse whisper, such as one often hears at camp-meeting: "Bless the Lord! O, bless the Lord!" She had the appearance of a lady in good circumstances, and a citizen informed me that she is ordinarily one of the quietest, most placid of women. One of her sons died of intemperance, and another is much addicted to liquor.

The eighteenth Amendment was ratified on January 29, 1919, and went into effect on January 29, 1920. Prohibition, however, did not stop millions of people from drinking. Americans flocked to establishments that sold alcohol illegally; these small, secretive clubs were nicknamed speakeasies because people often had to tell the guard at the door a password to gain entrance to them. The nation's continued thirst for alcohol helped make multimillionaires of criminals like Chicago's Al Capone, whose gangs illegally made, imported, and sold beer and liquor.

Prohibition simply did not work: Alcohol was still available for anyone who sought it. In *Drinking and Intoxication: Selected Readings in*

During Prohibition, people drank illegally in establishments known as speakeasies.

Social Attitudes and Controls, Raymond G. McCarthy says that although inadequate enforcement and public corruption were factors, the major reason Prohibition failed was because people refused to give up their drinks:

> It cannot be doubted that one element which would be essential for the successful enforcement of Prohibition was ultimately lacking—popular support. However much public sentiment the advocates of Prohibition had mustered in favor of the experiment before the Eighteenth Amendment was passed, sufficient popular support for its enforcement was not in evidence in the succeeding years.[77]

Support for Prohibition gradually weakened, and in 1932 the Democratic Party adopted a platform calling for repeal, which helped Democrat Franklin D. Roosevelt win election as president. In February 1933 Congress adopted the Twenty-first Amendment to the Constitution, which repealed the Eighteenth, and on December 5, 1933, Utah became the 36th state to vote for repeal, thus ratifying the amendment and ending Prohibition.

Although Prohibition failed, some good came from it. Prohibition shattered the old saloon system, which was considered responsible for much of the nation's alcohol abuse, and it helped curb America's previously spectacular drinking habit. The nation's per capita consumption of pure alcohol from 1906 to 1910 equaled 2.6 gallons, but after repeal of Prohibition in 1934 that figure had fallen to 0.97 of a gallon.

More Alcohol Woes

Although a few states continued to prohibit the sale of alcohol for many years (Kansas until 1948, Oklahoma until 1957, and Mississippi until 1966), most state and local governments turned to less strict measures to control alcohol abuse, such as banning the sale of alcohol on Sunday or only allowing government-operated establishments to dispense alcohol. In *Battling Demon Rum*, Thomas R. Pegram explains this less severe style of alcohol regulation:

> Although the new system was more uniform in practice and more efficient in enforcement, it nevertheless resembled the basic forms of liquor control practiced at the turn of the century: prohibition [in some counties alcohol is banned even today], government control of liquor sales through state stores, or a system of licenses, taxes, and regulations to monitor retail dealers.[78]

Not surprisingly, when Prohibition ended Americans gradually began to drink more again; by 1940 per capita consumption had increased to 1.56 gallons of pure alcohol, and by 1970 it was 2.61

gallons, slightly higher than the level before Prohibition. As the decades passed and increased drinking led to more and more alcohol-related problems, some people began to demand government action to control abusive drinkers.

MADD

The group that led the way for a return to stronger government intervention in alcohol problems was Mothers Against Drunk Driving (MADD). In May 1980, after her thirteen-year-old daughter, Cari, was killed by a drunk driver in Sacramento, California, Realtor Candy Lightner formed Mothers Against Drunk Drivers (*Drunk Drivers* was later changed to *Drunk Driving* in 1984). The driver of the car that killed Cari had received only minor punishment for a previous drunk-driving conviction, and Lightner decided that stronger drunk-driving laws were needed to make highways safe.

By the end of the year, Lightner had forced creation of a California Governor's Task Force on Drinking-Driving, launched the national movement known as MADD, and began to make people around the nation concerned about drunk driving and related alcohol problems. In *Contested Meanings: The Construction of Alcohol Problems,* Joseph R. Gusfield says the group galvanized the nation to act on this issue:

> The very name, MADD, presents the symbols that carry an expressive imagery. "Mothers" puts the issue in a framework of violence against children. "Against" provides an emotional sense of battles and enemies. "Drunk drivers" provides an image of the [driver] as socially irresponsible and out of self-control. This is the "killer drunk" who constitutes the villain of the story. . . . This capacity to characterize [drunk driving] as a drama of villains and victims has produced a moral fervor that moved the problem from its shadowy existence into the light of public mobilization.[79]

In 1982, the year in which MADD grew to one hundred chapters nationwide, there were 25,165 traffic fatalities linked to alcohol, 57.3 percent of the nearly forty-four thousand people killed in all crashes. But thanks to MADD and many other groups that joined the effort to fight drunk driving, lawmakers since then have passed tough new laws that have imposed much harsher penalties on offenders. Many of the new laws nationwide have greatly increased fines drunk drivers have to pay and have mandated that even first-time offenders must serve minimum jail sentences. These penalties are so much more se-

vere than under the old laws that they have helped to significantly reduce such deaths by making many people afraid to drive when they
are intoxicated. Many states also require drunk-driving offenders to
take a class on alcohol use or even attend meetings of Alcoholics
Anonymous.

In 1999 there were 41,611 traffic fatalities on the nation's roads,
but only 15,786, or 37.9 percent, involved drinking drivers. The new
regulations had begun working to get drunk drivers off the road.

The New Prohibition

The success the nation had in dealing with drunk driving convinced
some groups concerned about excessive drinking that they had a
chance to successfully fight what they considered to be other alcohol-
related problems, such as teenage drinking and the huge amount of

*Candy Lightner, the founder of Mothers Against Drunk Driving
(MADD), holds a picture of her daughter Cari. Her teenage daughter
was killed by a drunk driver in 1980.*

Beer advertisers have begun targeting younger viewers by featuring cartoon-like mascots in television commercials.

alcohol advertising on television. This phenomenon is known as "the New Prohibition."

One of the groups in this new movement is the Center for Science in the Public Interest (CSPI), a nonprofit education and advocacy organization. "It's improper to allow unfettered marketing of a product [alcohol] that causes 100,000 deaths a year,"[80] says CSPI executive director Michael F. Jacobson. The CSPI, which has eight hundred thousand subscribers to its newsletter, backs restrictions on advertising, higher taxes for alcoholic beverages, and greater efforts to reduce drinking by young people.

CSPI strongly believes that federal, state, and local governments need to do more to regulate companies that produce alcoholic beverages, specifically in the area of advertising: "The alcohol industry's relentless marketing and powerful political influence coupled with ineffective government alcohol policies, contribute to this ongoing public health and safety epidemic."[81]

The efforts to control alcohol advertising take many forms. Senator Strom Thurmond of South Carolina, for example, has tried to stop wine makers from claiming on their labels that drinking wine is healthy, the city of Los Angeles has banned outdoor advertising of alcoholic beverages, and the CSPI wants to bar alcohol ads on television until after 10:00 P.M. so that fewer young people see such commercials.

Youth Drinking

Of all of the efforts to regulate alcohol today, more are aimed at illegal underage drinkers than any other group. That is because teenage drinking is one of the nation's biggest alcohol problems. Although the legal drinking age in America was once eighteen, it has been twenty-one for several decades. Despite that, many young people drink. In 2000 a U.S. Department of Health and Human Services study on underage drinking showed that 30 percent of twelfth graders, 26.2 percent of tenth graders, and 14.1 percent of eighth graders reported binge drinking at least once in the two weeks prior to the survey; binge drinking was defined as five or more drinks on one occasion.

To many people, one of the most troubling aspects of underage drinking is the exposure young people get to alcohol through advertisements. The alcohol industry spends more than $1 billion a year on advertising, much of it on television shows involving sporting events that young people avidly watch. In a 1999 report on underage drinking and advertising, the Federal Trade Commission (FTC) said,

> Underage alcohol use is a significant national concern. Last year [1998], a third of twelfth graders reported binge drinking. Moreover, while underage alcohol use levels decreased from about 1980 to 1993, those decreases have stopped and some important markers of underage alcohol use appear to be on the rise. Finding ways to deter alcohol use by those under 21 is a constant challenge to the beverage alcohol industry . . . as well as for government agencies and consumer [groups].[82]

Partly because it has not been proven that advertising directly increases underage alcohol consumption, the FTC recommended the industry continue to self-regulate its marketing to avoid appealing to younger people. But the fact that young people are exposed to such ads, as well as to examples of alcohol use in movies and other mass media, is a big concern. Former surgeon general David Satcher believes

Eleanor Mill. Reprinted by permission of Mill News Art Syndicate.

the problem of underage drinking has become worse because drinkers are getting younger and younger:

> There was a time when alcohol use was considered a "rite of passage," however, that "passage" was from adolescence into adulthood. Today as we see younger and younger children using alcohol, the "passage" is too frequently from childhood into adolescence. We now know that children who begin drinking alcohol before the age of 15 are four times more likely to develop alcoholism in adulthood than those children who do not begin consuming alcohol until the legal age of 21.[83]

Part of Life

The controversy over alcohol advertising is only one of the many concerns Americans have over the very real dangers that alcohol poses to society. However, the fact that alcohol is such an important part of life for so many millions of people means that any attempt to regulate it will always meet with resistance. Marc Schuckit, a psychiatrist and addiction specialist who teaches at the University of California at San Diego School of Medicine, explains this situation:

> It's part of our culture. People accept it as a normal part of our culture and dance around the issue [of alcohol's danger] by saying that everyone's at risk but me. When you have something that's been in your society so long and so tolerated, it's hard even to stop and think about the risks that are involved.[84]

Notes

Intoduction: It Touches Everyone

1. Quoted in National Institute on Alcohol Abuse and Alcoholism, *Alcoholism*. www.niaaa.nih.gov/publications/booklet-text.html.
2. Quoted in John Lawson, *Friends You Can Drop: Alcohol and Other Drugs*. Boston: Quinlan, 1986, p. 1.

Chapter 1: A History of Alcohol Use

3. Alice Fleming, *Alcohol: The Delightful Poison*. New York: Delacorte, 1975, p. 3.
4. Quoted in Edith Lisansky Gomberg, Helene Rakkin White, and John A. Carpenter, eds., *Alcohol, Science, and Society Revisited*. Ann Arbor: University of Michigan Press, 1982, p. 73.
5. Quoted in Fleming, *Alcohol*, p. 100.
6. Quoted in Wolfgang Schivelbusch, *Tastes of Paradise: A Social History of Spices, Stimulants, and Intoxicants*. New York: Pantheon Books, 1992, p. 22.
7. Quoted in Raymond G. McCarthy, ed., *Drinking and Intoxication: Selected Readings in Social Attitudes and Controls*. Binghampton, NY: Vail-Ballou, Inc., 1959, p. 15.
8. Quoted in Fleming, *Alcohol*, p. 12.
9. Quoted in Fleming, *Alcohol*, p. 113.
10. Quoted in David T. Courtwright, *Forces of Habit: Drugs and the Making of the Modern World*. Cambridge, MA: Harvard University Press, 2001, p. 72.
11. Quoted in Thomas Szasz, *Ceremonial Chemistry: The Ritual Persecution of Drugs, Addicts, and Pushers*. New York: Anchor/Doubleday, 1974, p. 44.
12. Don Cahalan, *Understanding America's Drinking Problem: How to Combat the Hazards of Alcohol*. San Francisco: Jossey-Bass, 1987, p. 25.
13. Quoted in J. C. Furnas, *The Life and Times of the Late Demon Rum*. New York: J. P. Putnam's Sons, 1965, p. 347.

14. Schivelbusch, *Tastes of Paradise*, p. 153.
15. Quoted in Schivelbusch, *Tastes of Paradise*, p. 155.
16. Quoted in Mark Edward Lender and James Kirby Martin, *Drinking in America: A History*. New York: Free, 1987, p. 15.

Chapter 2: Alcohol's Effect on the Body

17. James R. Milam and Katherine Ketcham, *Under the Influence: A Guide to the Myths and Realities of Alcoholism*. Seattle, WA: Madrona, 1981, p. 16.
18. *Tenth Special Report to the U.S. Congress on Alcohol and Health*. Washington, DC: National Institutes of Health, Publication no. 00-1583, 2000, p. 67.
19. *Tenth Special Report to the U.S. Congress on Alcohol and Health*, p. 69.
20. Katherine Ketcham and William F. Asbury, *Beyond the Influence: Understanding and Defeating Alcoholism*. New York: Bantam Books, 2000, p. 30.
21. Milt, *Alcoholism*, p. 10.
22. Quoted in Joseph R. Gusfield, *Contested Meanings: The Construction of Alcohol Problems*. Madison: University of Wisconsin Press, 1996, p. 53.
23. Gail Gleason Milgram, "The Effects of Alcohol," fact sheet no. 15, 1996. www.rci.rutgers.edu/~cas2/facts.html.
24. Mark S. Gold, *The Facts About Drugs and Alcohol*, 3rd ed. New York: Bantam Books, 1988, p. 76.

Chapter 3: Alcohol Abuse and Addiction

25. Margaret O. Hyde, *Addictions: Gambling, Smoking, Cocaine Use, and Others*. New York: McGraw-Hill, 1978, p. 87.
26. E. M. Jellinek, *The Disease Concept of Alcoholism*. New Brunswick, NJ: Hillhouse, 1960, p. 35.
27. Quoted in Dagobert D. Runes, ed., *The Selected Writings of Benjamin Rush*. New York: Philosophical Library, 1947, p. 337.
28. *Tenth Special Report to the U.S. Congress on Alcohol and Health*, p. xiii.
29. Quoted in Public Broadcasting System, "Close to Home," March 29, 1998. www.pbs.org/wnet/closetohome/science/index.html.
30. Alan I. Leshner, "Oops: How Casual Drug Use Leads to Addiction." http://165.112.78.61/Published_Articles/Oops.html.

31. Quoted in "Do You Think You're Different?" New York: Alcoholics Anonymous World Services, 1976, p. 9.
32. Quoted in Public Broadcasting System, "Close to Home."
33. Quoted in Hazelden Foundation, "Addiction: A Brain Disease with Biological Underpinnings." www.hazelden.org/newsletter_detail.dbm?ID=1104.
34. Quoted in C. W. Henderson, "Alcoholism Is Result of Genetic and Environmental Factors," *Genomics and Genetics Weekly*, March 9, 2001, p. 24+.
35. David J. Hanson, "Advertising, Consumption, and Abuse." www2.potsdam.edu/alcohol-info/Advertising/Advertising.html.
36. Quoted in E. M. Pattison and E. Kaufman, *Encyclopedic Handbook of Alcoholism*. New York: Gardner, 1982, p. 438.
37. Quoted in "Do You Think You're Different?" p. 16.
38. Milam and Ketcham, *Under the Influence*, p. 30.
39. Quoted in Bob B., "Thinking About Drinking," *AA Grapevine*, September 1997, p. 15.
40. Milt, *Alcoholism*, p. 54.
41. Quoted in Ketcham and Asbury, *Beyond the Influence*, p. 53.

Chapter 4: How Alcohol Ruins Lives

42. Quoted in Leshner, "Oops."
43. Quoted in Public Broadcasting System, "Close to Home."
44. John, interview with author, September 15, 2001. (*Author's note:* The names of recovering alcoholics interviewed for this book have been changed.)
45. Quoted in Susan Brink, "Your Brain on Alcohol," *U.S. News & World Report*, May 7, 2001, p. 50+.
46. Quoted in Brink, "Your Brain on Alcohol."
47. Jim, interview with author, September 17, 2001.
48. Jerry, interview with author, September 15, 2001.
49. Milt, *Alcoholism*, p. 10.
50. Quoted in Brink, "Your Brain on Alcohol," p50+.
51. Quoted in "Do You Think You're Different?" p. 14.
52. Quoted in Public Broadcasting System, "Close to Home."
53. *Tenth Special Report to the U.S. Congress on Alcohol and Health*, p. 56.
54. Joe, interview with author, September 17, 2001.
55. Quoted in M. O. Berman, "Alcoholic Korsakoff's Syndrome," *Alcohol Health and Research World*, vol. 14, issue 2, 1990, p. 120+.

56. Nasdijj, "The Blood Runs Like a River Through My Dreams," *Esquire,* June 1999, p. 115+.
57. Nasdijj, "The Blood Runs Like a River Through My Dreams," p. 115+.
58. Quoted in Brink, "Your Brain on Alcohol," p. 50+.

Chapter 5: Alcohol: Treating the Disease

59. Nan Robertson, *Getting Better: Inside Alcoholics Anonymous.* New York: William Morrow, 1988, p. 32.
60. Quoted in Jellinek, *The Disease Concept of Alcoholism,* p. 210.
61. Quoted in Gusfield, *Contested Meanings,* p. 205.
62. Quoted in Hazelden Foundation, "Breaking Through Denial Is Alcoholic's First Step in Recovery, *Alive and Free.* www.hazelden. org/newsletter_detail.html.
63. Quoted in Chris, "The All-American Housewife," *AA Grapevine,* August 2000, p. 10.
64. Quoted in Ketcham and Asbury, *Beyond the Influence,* p. 139.
65. Jane, interview with author, September 20, 2001.
66. *Forty-four Questions.* New York: Alcoholics Anonymous World Services, 1952, p. 19.
67. "Is There an Alcoholic in Your Life? AA's Message of Hope." New York: Alcoholics Anonymous World Services, 1976, p. 1.
68. *Columbia University College of Physicians and Surgeons Complete Home Medical Guide.* www.cpmcnet.columbia.edu/texts/guide/ toc/toc06.html.
69. Arnold M. Ludwig, *Understanding the Alcoholic's Mind: The Nature of Craving and How to Control It.* New York: Oxford University Press, 1988, p. 112.
70. Nicholas A. Pace, "Interviews with the Experts." www.ncadd.org/ facts/pace.html.
71. *Tenth Special Report to the U.S. Congress on Alcohol and Health,* p. 448.

Chapter 6: A History of Regulation

72. Quoted in Gail Gleason Milgram and the Editors of Consumer Reports Books, *The Facts About Drinking: Coping with Alcohol Use, Abuse, and Alcoholism.* Mount Vernon, NY: Consumers Union of United States, Inc., 1990, p. 1.
73. Cahalan, *Understanding America's Drinking Problem,* p. 24.
74. Quoted in Fleming, *Alcohol,* p. 66.

75. Quoted in Thomas R. Pegram, *Battling Demon Rum: The Struggle for a Dry America, 1800–1933*. Chicago: Ivan R. Dee, 1998, p. 17.
76. Quoted in Furnas, *The Life and Times of the Late Demon Rum*, p. 35.
77. Quoted in McCarthy, *Drinking and Intoxication*, p. 379.
78. Quoted in Pegram, *Battling Demon Rum*, p. 186.
79. Quoted in Gusfield, *Contested Meanings*, p. 311.
80. Quoted in Joyce Howard Price, "'Neo-Prohibitionists' Want Greater Regulation of Alcohol," *Insight on the News*, February 1, 1999, p. 20+.
81. Center for Science in the Public Interest, "CSPI National Alcohol Policies Project." www.cspinet.org/booze/pdbooze.html.
82. Quoted in Janet M. Evans and Richard F. Kelly, "A Review of Industry Efforts to Avoid Promoting Alcohol to Underage Consumers," September 1999. www.ftc.gov/reports/alcohol/alcoholreport.html.
83. David Satcher, "Surgeon General David Satcher, MD, PhD, on Binge Drinking." www.ncadd.org/programs/awareness/satcher.html.
84. Quoted in Public Broadcasting System, "Close to Home."

Organizations to Contact

Al-Anon and Alateen
PO Box 262, Midtown Station
New York, NY 10018
(800) 344-2666
website: www.al-anon.alateen.org

Al-Anon is a fellowship of men, women, and children whose lives have been affected by an alcoholic family member or friend. Members share their experiences, strength, and hope with one another to help each other and perhaps to aid in the recovery of the alcoholic. A source of information on how to help people cope with this disease and listings for Al-Anon meetings around the nation. It was started by Lois Wilson, wife of one of the founders of Alcoholics Anonymous.

Alateen is a fellowship of young people who share their experiences, strength, and hope with one another to help each other recover from alcoholism. It is based on the principles of Alcoholics Anonymous.

Alcoholics Anonymous (AA)
Grand Central Station
PO Box 459
New York, NY 10163
(212) 870-3400
website: www.aa.org
Alcoholics Anonymous is a worldwide fellowship of alcoholics who share their experiences, strength, and hope with one another to help each other recover from alcoholism. Its primary purpose is to carry the message of AA to other alcoholics. AA publishes many pamphlets and books on alcoholism and its twelve-step program. Several AA pamphlets can be downloaded from its Internet site.

Hazelden Foundation
PO Box 176
15251 Pleasant Valley Rd.
Center City, MN 55012-9640
(800) 329-9000
website: www.hazelden.org

A nonprofit organization dedicated to helping people recover from alcoholism. It publishes pamphlets and books on recovery from alcoholism. Its Internet site is a valuable source of information on alcohol, its history, and the disease of alcoholism.

Mothers Against Drunk Driving (MADD)
511 E. John Carpenter Fwy. Suite 700
Irving, TX 75062
(800) GET-MADD
website: www.madd.org

MADD has been fighting for over two decades to reduce problems associated with drinking and driving. Its Internet site has the latest information on this topic as well as current drunk-driving laws and attempts to strengthen them.

National Council on Alcoholism and Drug Dependence (NCADD)
12 W. 21st St.
New York, NY 10010
(800) NCA-CALL
website: www.ncadd.org

Founded in 1944 by Marty Mann, the first woman to find long-term sobriety in Alcoholics Anonymous, the NCADD provides education, information, and help to the public about the disease of alcoholism.

National Institute on Alcohol Abuse and Alcoholism (NIAAA)
Wilco Bldg.
6000 Executive Blvd., Suite 409
Bethesda, MD 20892-7003
(301) 443-3860
website: www.niaaa.nih.gov

The NIAAA is part of the National Institutes of Health. It supports and conducts biomedical and behavioral research on the causes, consequences, treatments, and prevention of alcohol and alcohol-related problems. It publishes a great deal of information on alcohol and alcoholism, and its Internet site is a wonderful source of information and statistics on the subjects of alcohol and alcoholism.

National Institute on Drug Abuse (NIDA)
6001 Executive Blvd., Room 5213
Bethesda, MD 20892-9651
(301) 443-1124
website: www.nida.nih.gov

Part of the National Institutes of Health, NIDA researches and provides information and help to the public on alcoholism and other drug abuse. Its Internet site is a valuable source of information on addiction and recovery.

National Organization on Fetal Alcohol Syndrome (NOFAS)
216 G St. N.E.
Washington, DC 20002
(202) 785-4585
website: www.nofas.org

NOFAS is a nonprofit organization founded in 1990 dedicated to eliminating birth defects caused by alcohol consumption during pregnancy and improving the quality of life for those individuals and families affected. It offers information on the issue and where to find help locally.

Substance Abuse and Mental Health Services Administration (SAMHSA)
5600 Fishers Ln.
Rockville, MD 20857
(301) 443-6239
website: www.samhsa.org

The SAMHSA is the federal agency charged with improving the quality and availability of prevention, treatment, and rehabilitative services in order to reduce illness, death, disability, and cost to society resulting from substance abuse and mental illnesses. Its Internet site has a lot of good information on alcohol and treatment for alcoholism, including statistics from federal surveys on alcohol use.

For Further Reading

Don Cahalan, *Understanding America's Drinking Problem: How to Combat the Hazards of Alcohol*. San Francisco: Jossey-Bass, 1987. The author ably explains the history of drinking in America.

Alice Fleming, *Alcohol: The Delightful Poison*. New York: Delacorte, 1975. An informative, colorful history of alcohol use throughout history.

Mark S. Gold, *The Good News About Drugs and Alcohol*. New York: Villard Books, 1991. Gold, a doctor, explains how alcohol and other drugs harm people and how they can be treated for their addiction.

Katherine Ketcham and William F. Asbury, *Beyond the Influence: Understanding and Defeating Alcoholism*. New York: Bantam Books, 2000. A well-written, informative discussion of the disease of alcoholism.

Cynthia Kuhn, Scott Swartzwelder, and Wilkie Wilson, *Buzzed: The Straight Facts About the Most Used and Abused Drugs from Alcohol to Ecstacy*. New York: W. W. Norton, 1998. Although it deals with addiction to a variety of drugs, the section on alcohol is excellent.

Marty Mann, *Marty Mann Answers Your Questions About Drinking and Alcoholism*. New York: Holt, Rinehart & Winston, 1981. Mann, a recovering alcoholic, discusses the subject in a question-and-answer format that makes the information easy to absorb.

Harry Milt, *Alcoholism, Its Causes and Cure: A New Handbook*. New York: Charles Scribner's Sons, 1976. An informative book about alcohol and how people become addicted to it.

National Institute on Alcohol Abuse and Alcoholism, "Alcohol: Getting the Facts." www.niaaa.nih.gov/publications/booklet. It contains easy to understand explanations about basic questions people have concerning alcohol use and alcoholism.

Works Consulted

Books

Alcoholics Anonymous. 3rd ed. New York: Alcoholics Anonymous World Services, 1976. The book that helped introduce AA to the world and explains its twelve-step program of recovery.

David T. Courtwright, *Forces of Habit: Drugs and the Making of the Modern World.* Cambridge, MA: Harvard University Press, 2001. A scholarly look at how drugs spread around the world and helped shape its development.

J. C. Furnas, *The Life and Times of the Late Demon Rum.* New York: J. P. Putnam's Sons, 1965. An amusing but insightful study of the Temperance Movement.

Kathlyn Gay and Martin K. Gay, *Encylopedia of North American Eating and Drinking Traditions, Customs and Rituals.* Santa Barbara, CA: ABC-CLIO, 1996. It explains the social aspects that have grown up around eating and drinking.

Mark S. Gold, *The Facts About Drugs and Alcohol.* 3rd ed. New York: Bantam Books, 1988. A basic explanation of alcohol, other drugs, and addiction in general.

Edith Lisansky Gomberg, Helene Rakkin White, and John A. Carpenter, eds., *Alcohol, Science, and Society Revisited.* Ann Arbor: University of Michigan Press, 1982. A collection of academic studies on alcohol.

Joseph R. Gusfield, *Contested Meanings: The Construction of Alcohol Problems.* Madison: University of Wisconsin Press, 1996. A philosophical discussion about how society perceives and handles alcohol problems.

D. B. Heath, ed., *International Handbook on Alcohol and Culture.* Westport, CT: Greenwood, 1995. A collection of articles on various aspects of alcohol and drinking.

Margaret O. Hyde, *Addictions: Gambling, Smoking, Cocaine Use, and Others.* New York: McGraw-Hill, 1978. It discusses how addiction works in regard to alcohol and other catalysts.

Brian Inglis, *The Forbidden Game: A Social History of Drugs.* New York: Charles Scribner's Sons, 1975. The author investigates how drugs have affected culture and how attitudes toward them have shifted over the centuries.

E. M. Jellinek, *The Disease Concept of Alcoholism.* New Brunswick, NJ: Hillhouse, 1960. The groundbreaking work that helped alcoholism become recognized as a disease.

Mark Edward Lender and James Kirby Martin, *Drinking in America: A History.* New York: Free, 1987. The authors describe how drinking patterns have evolved throughout U.S. history.

Arnold M. Ludwig, *Understanding the Alcoholic's Mind: The Nature of Craving and How to Control It.* New York: Oxford University Press, 1988. A psychiatrist's interpretation of how a drinker's psychological makeup contributes to addiction.

Raymond G. McCarthy, ed., *Drinking and Intoxication: Selected Readings in Social Attitudes and Controls.* Binghampton, NY: Vail-Ballou, 1959. Scholarly works on alcohol, its history, and how it addicts people.

James R. Milam and Katherine Ketcham, *Under the Influence: A Guide to the Myths and Realities of Alcoholism.* Seattle, WA: Madrona, 1981. A solid explanation of how alcohol works and the disease of alcoholism.

Gail Gleason Milgram and the Editors of Consumer Reports Books, *The Facts About Drinking: Coping with Alcohol Use, Abuse, and Alcoholism.* Mount Vernon, NY: Consumers Union of United States, 1990. A well-written book that can help people deal with the disease.

E. M. Pattison and E. Kaufman, *Encyclopedic Handbook of Alcoholism.* New York: Gardner, 1982. A collection of articles on various aspects of alcohol and alcoholism.

Thomas R. Pegram, *Battling Demon Rum: The Struggle for a Dry America, 1800–1933.* Chicago: Ivan R. Dee, 1998. An entertaining, revealing study of the relationship between politics and the Temperance Movement.

Nan Robertson, *Getting Better: Inside Alcoholics Anonymous.* New York: William Morrow, 1988. A discussion of Alcoholics

Anonymous, the group that helped this former *New York Times* reporter quit drinking.

James E. Royce, *Alcohol Problems and Alcoholism: A Comprehensive Survey.* New York: Free, 1981. A review of all aspects of this disease.

Dagobert D. Runes, *The Selected Writings of Benjamin Rush.* New York: Philosophical Library, 1947. A collection of the written works by one of early America's most original social commentators.

Wolfgang Schivelbusch, *Tastes of Paradise: A Social History of Spices, Stimulants, and Intoxicants.* New York: Pantheon Books, 1992. Translated from the original German by David Jacobson, this is an amusing, informative look at how alcohol, coffee, and other drinks became popular.

Thomas Szasz, *Ceremonial Chemistry: The Ritual Persecution of Drugs, Addicts, and Pushers.* New York: Anchor/Doubleday, 1974. The author looks at how alcoholics and other addicts have been treated by society.

Tenth Special Report to the U.S. Congress on Alcohol and Health. Washington, DC: National Institutes of Health, Publication no. 00-1583, 2000. A report by the National Institutes of Health and National Institute on Alcohol Abuse and Alcoholism that summarizes U.S. research on alcohol and alcoholism.

Joseph Volpicelli and Maia Szalavitz, *Recovery Options: The Complete Guide.* New York: John Wiley & Sons, Inc., 2000. The authors discuss all phases of recovery from addiction to alcohol and other drugs.

Janet Geringer Woititz, *Adult Children of Alcoholics.* Pompano Beach, FL: Health Communications, 1983. A discussion of how growing up in an alcoholic family harms children.

Periodicals

Alcohol Research and Health, "Why Do Some People Drink Too Much?" vol. 24, issue 1, January 2000.

Bob B., "Thinking About Drinking," *AA Grapevine,* September 1997.

M. O. Berman, "Alcoholic Korsakoff's Syndrome," *Alcohol Health and Research World,* vol. 14, issue 2, 1990.

Susan Brink, "Your Brain on Alcohol," *U.S. News & World Report,* May 7, 2001.

James Carroll, "Ensuring Safe Roads," *State Government News,* February 2001.

Susan Cheever, "The Healer Bill W.," *Time,* June 14, 1999.

Chris, "The All-American Housewife," *AA Grapevine,* August 2000.

Current Events, "New Preliminary Studies Link Teen Alcohol Abuse to Brain Damage," November 17, 2000.

Richard K. Fuller and Susanne Hiller-Sturmhöfel, "Alcoholism Treatment in the United States," *Alcohol Research and Health,* February 1999.

C. W. Henderson, "Alcoholism Is Result of Genetic and Environmental Factors," *Genomics and Genetics Weekly,* March 9, 2001.

Charles Krauthhammer, "The New Prohibitionism," *Time,* October 6, 1997.

Norman S. Miller, "Management of Withdrawal Syndromes and Relapse Prevention in Drug and Alcohol Dependence," *American Family Physician,* July 1998.

Nasdijj, "The Blood Runs Like a River Through My Dreams," *Esquire,* June 1999, p. 115+.

Robert Nash Parker and Kathleen Auerhahn, "Alcohol, Drugs, and Violence," *Annual Review of Sociology,* 1998.

Joyce Howard Price, "'Neo-Prohibitionists' Want Greater Regulation of Alcohol," *Insight on the News,* February 1, 1999.

Peter Provet, "Drinking in Moderation Is Not an Option for Alcoholics," *Alcoholism and Drug Abuse Weekly,* July 31, 2000.

Joan Raymond et al., "Can This Pill Stop You from Hitting the Bottle?" *Newsweek,* February 12, 2001.

Bernice Wuethrich, "Getting Stupid," *Discover,* March 2001.

Pamphlets

"Do You Think You're Different?" New York: Alcoholics Anonymous World Services, 1976.

"Forty-four Questions." New York: Alcoholics Anonymous World Services, 1952.

"Is There an Alcoholic in Your Life? AA's Message of Hope." New York: Alcoholics Anonymous World Services, 1976.

National Council on Alcoholism and Drug Dependence, "Facts on Alcohol." www.ncadd.org/facts/defalc.html.

National Institute on Alcohol Abuse and Alcoholism, "Alcohol: What You Don't Know Can Harm You." www.niaaa.nih.gov/publications/harm-al.html.

——— "Alcoholism: Getting the Facts." www.niaaa.nih.gov/publications/booklet-text.html.

Television
Public Broadcasting System, "Close to Home," March 29, 1998. www.pbs.org/wnet/closetohome/html.

Internet Sources
American Society of Addictive Medicine Board of Directors, "The Use of Alcohol and Other Drugs During Pregnancy," November 6, 1988. www.asam.org/ppol/Contents.html.

Center for Science in the Public Interest, "CSPI National Alcohol Policies Project." www.cspinet.org/booze/pdbooze.html.

Columbia University College of Physicians and Surgeons Complete Home Medical Guide. www.cpmcnet.columbia.edu/texts/guide/toc/toc06.html.

Janet M. Evans and Richard F. Kelly, "A Review of Industry Efforts to Avoid Promoting Alcohol to Underage Consumers," September 1999. www.ftc.gov/reports/alcohol/alcoholreport.html.

David J. Hanson, "Advertising, Consumption, and Abuse." www2.potsdam.edu/alcohol-info/Advertising/Advertising.html.

Hazelden Foundation, "Addiction: A Brain Disease with Biological Underpinnings." www.hazelden.org/newsletter_detail.dbm?ID=1104.

———, "Breaking Through Denial Is Alcoholic's First Step in Recovery," *Alive and Free.* www.hazelden.org/newsletter_detail.html.

Alan I. Leshner, "Oops: How Casual Drug Use Leads to Addiction." http://165.112.78.61/Published_Articles/Oops.html.

Gail Gleason Milgram, "The Effects of Alcohol," fact sheet no. 15, 1996. www.rci.rutgers.edu/~cas2/facts.html.

National Institute on Alcohol Abuse and Alcoholism, "Alcohol Metabolism," *Alcohol Alert No. 35,* January 1997. www.niaaa.nih.gov/publications/aa35.html.

Ohio State University History Department, "Temperance and Prohibition." www.history.ohio-state.edu/projects/prohibition.html.

Nicholas A. Pace, "Interviews with the Experts." www.ncadd.org/facts/pace.html.

Thomas A. Pearson, "Alcohol and Heart Disease." www.americanheart.org/Scientific/statements/1996/1116.ht.

David Satcher, "Surgeon General David Satcher, MD, PhD, on Binge Drinking." www.ncadd.org/programs/awareness/satcher.html.

Substance Abuse and Mental Health Services Administration, "1999 National Household Survey on Drug Abuse (NHSDA)." www.samhsa.gov/oas/NHSDA/1999.

Joseph R. Volpicelli, "Alcohol Dependence: Diagnosis, Clinical Aspects, and Biopsychosocial Causes," 1997. www.uncg.edu/edu/ericcass/substnce/docs/dependen.html.

Robert Westermeyer, "Blood Alcohol Level (BAL) Monitoring." www.habitsmart.com/bal.html.

Index

Picture Credits

About the Author

Michael V. Uschan has written sixteen books on a wide variety of subjects, including biographies of president John F. Kennedy, Tiger Woods, and Minnesota governor Jesse Ventura. Mr. Uschan began his career as a writer and editor with United Press International, a wire service that provided stories to newspapers, radio, and television. Journalism is sometimes called "history in a hurry." Mr. Uschan considers writing history books a natural extension of skills he developed in his many years as a working journalist. He and his wife, Barbara, reside in the Milwaukee suburb of Franklin, Wisconsin.